Carolina Autumn

ALSO BY CAROL LYNCH WILLIAMS

Kelly and Me

Adeline Street

The True Colors of Caitlynne Jackson

If I Forget, You Remember

My Angelica

Carolina Autumn

CAROL LYNCH WILLIAMS

DELACORTE PRESS

Published by
Delacorte Press
an imprint of
Random House Children's Books
a division of Random House, Inc.
1540 Broadway
New York, New York 10036

Visit us on the Web! www.randomhouse.com/kids
Educators and librarians, for a variety of teaching tools, visit us at
www.randomhouse.com/teachers

Library of Congress Cataloging-in-Publication Data

Williams, Carol Lynch.
   Carolina autumn/by Carol Lynch Williams.
      p. cm.
   Summary: As she begins high school, fourteen-year-old Carolina tries to come
to terms with the death of her father and older sister, while dealing with diffi-
cult relationships with her mother and best friend and a budding romance
with the boy next door.
   ISBN 0-385-32716-1
   [1. Death—Fiction. 2. Grief—Fiction. 3. Mothers and daughters—Fiction.
4. Sisters—Fiction. 5. Interpersonal relations—Fiction] I. Title.

PZ7.W65588 Car 2000
[Fic]—dc21   99-089837

The text of this book is set in 13-point Garamond 3.
Book design by Debora Smith
Manufactured in the United States of America
September 2000
10 9 8 7 6 5 4 3 2 1
BVG

To my own sweet Carolina —
who came to us in the autumn

Carolina Autumn

Prologue

A Note to You

Have you ever had one of those times? You know the kind I'm talking about. It lasts forever, your whole life it seems, with very few ups and so many downs you feel like you've sunk lower into Mother Earth than a miner. And when you try to figure things out it's like putting together a puzzle when you know pieces are missing. Once everything's stuck all together you see that the most important part, your heart, was left out someplace, probably on the back steps in a storm.

That's what happened to me. Not me all alone. I mean, there's Mom too. But I'm the one who ended up with my heart all out of joint. Some because of the three of us: me and Poindexter and Mara Roberts. Mostly, well, mostly I need to tell you the whole story, from the beginning when my first day of bad days began. That way you can see it all for yourself.

Chapter 1

It started when I had to go and buy a bra but didn't. That was just this past spring, even though it seems years ago now. What an uncomfortable time of life. If Mom had been coherent she would have said to me, "Carolina, you're beginning to develop. Developing girls need bras. Let's go to Neiman's and see what we can find in the girls' section."

Then I would have changed my undershirt and put a clean T-shirt over the top of it so I'd be at least presentable from the waist up, and we would have left.

Of course, that didn't happen.

But I know it *would* have because that is the very thing Mom said to Madelaine when she got the beginnings of breasts. I was listening in, so I know for a fact. Mom said, "Madelaine, you're beginning to develop, and developing girls need bras."

"To lift and separate." That was me speaking from my hiding place outside the partway-opened door of my sister's room.

"Carolina," Madelaine had screeched. She leapt from the bed and slammed the door closed tight, just missing my nose.

Mom had started talking again, her voice a comfort to my sister, and when they left, Mom gave me a wink and said in a reassuring voice, "Your day will come."

"Gross," I had said.

And I felt that way still. Now. Gross.

One day I had been fine, running in the neighborhood with all my friends, wrestling with the guys, smacking a ball farther than any other batter. Then it seemed like the very next day. . . . I mean that, the *Very Next Day,* I was developing. Trying to move my arms without the feel of worrisome breasts-to-be. Running became a little painful. And to be bumped in the chest in a tackle, well, enough said.

By this time, though, Dad and Madelaine had gone on their little trip and they weren't coming back.

To make matters worse, Mom immersed herself in her job. And when my Beginning began, I just wore Madelaine's old undershirts, because by now it was plain to me that she and Dad weren't coming home. And in a way, Mom wasn't either.

It was Mara who tried to ground me. You know, give me a bit of comfort.

◐ ◐ ◐

A Note to You

All right, all right, we've always had differences here, but Mara has been a good friend for a long time. She looks as good as she used to, too. Her hair is so blond that it seems like the color of the fringes of a hot sun. And her eyes are that lavender that you only read about. I'm sure she's sincere, and it's the God's honest truth she's been here for me. And for a while there, I hung on to her fast and hard. Telling her every bitter thing that happened in my life, 'cause I couldn't find anything good. She was the lifeline to my memories. But back to the story. To the beginning.

Mara pulled me aside in her room. "Carolina," she whispered, "it's finally *happening* to you." She looked at me chest level, and me being the self-conscious type when it came to my body, I crossed my arms to cover myself.

"What?" I asked, though I knew darn good and well what she was talking about. How could I not? She practically shined a spotlight on the exact places she was gawking at. And it wasn't like I hadn't noticed what crazy things were going on.

"Bosoms." She pointed with her chin. Twice.

"So?" *So* is a good answer anytime you don't really have a good answer.

Mara smiled at me. "You're fourteen."

"I had been wondering about my age. I was confused. But thank you for setting me straight."

Mara heaved a sigh big as her own chest, which, by the way, began to develop when she was eleven and a half. I remember it happened over the summer. And so does everyone who was in our class when school started. Or in the hall during change of periods. Or out on the ball field.

"You've been wearing an undershirt now for too long. Everybody's wearing bras."

I tilted my head down and looked at Mara through my bangs. "Poindexter doesn't wear a bra. Or Matt or Christian or—"

"Ha ha, very funny."

I had to be funny. This was my *body* she was talking about. "Well, not everybody wears a bra, though you'd probably agree with me if I said Mr. Holliday needs one."

Mr. Holliday taught us eighth-grade math the year before.

Mara laughed. "You're changing the subject, Carolina, like you always do."

I grinned. The year was a bad one, what with Dad and Madelaine leaving like they did and these things called breasts making their way into my world. But Mara was a good part of my life, laughing at the things I said that were funny, and just being there for me.

"You need a bra, Carolina." Mara walked over to her dresser and opened a drawer. "Now lookit here. I've outgrown all these years ago."

Now it was my turn to laugh. "Years?" I asked in a sarcastic voice.

"It seems so," Mara said, and she pulled out bras in a huge array of colors: black, pink, cream, white, green, red, all of them shiny, all of them in a progression of sizes.

"If you'd let me talk to you before now, you could have worn a few of these flatter ones."

I dropped my mouth in mock horror.

"But since you didn't," Mara continued, talking like my face wasn't contorting right in front of her, "you'll have a smaller number to choose from. You've outgrown the starter bras."

I stood up and went to Mara's dresser too. "I'm doing fine with Madelaine's leftover undershirts," I said.

Mara opened her mouth and closed it a few times. There is an unspoken rule that she and I don't talk about Dad's abrupt leaving or the fact that he took Madelaine with him.

"Carolina," she said, closing the drawer, "take my advice. You need a bra. I'm telling you this as a best friend. You need support." Mara said the last three words like she was doing a commercial and waved a shiny bra at me.

So I took her word, and I took her leftover bras, and for the rest of the summer I wore them over Madelaine's left-behind undershirts because it seemed right, and because that way the bras didn't itch.

In my dreams I am like my mother before she changed. I am funny and, when it's necessary, I am serious. And while I look a lot like my father, I am mostly like Madelaine. That soft part of Madelaine, and the screaming part of her too, though I rarely get to let my screams out at all.

Chapter

Poindexter, my best guy friend in all the world, left for two months to do some kind of Exchange a Kid Around the World thing. That was at the beginning of this summer. He went to France.

I missed him awful, and since that's true I need to tell you about Poindexter.

A Note to You

Poindexter is the kind of guy anyone would approve of. He's clean-cut, his hair just a little long, and it's a yellowish brownish color. It curls a bit, especially on hot days, right up close to his face. Maybe on cooler days it curls up too. But I never really took the time to notice until this past summer, right before he left. Isn't that funny how I always do that, wait a little too long? It seems like I am always catching the beauty of something a moment too late.

First of all his real name is Garret Harrison and he's lived next door to us since Mom and I moved here.

"A change, Carolina," Mom had said. "We need a change."

I didn't want to leave our old home. Yes, there were memories stuck in every corner. To Mom those memories were painful. To me, they were a sore comfort, letting me know Dad and Madelaine were close even though they had taken off.

We changed houses, though we stayed in the general area so I'd still go to the same school, still be near to Mara. And to make things even a little nicer I got to be friends with Garret. I gave him the name Poindexter because of his hair: it stuck up in the back some, reminding me of a cartoon character I had scribbled once with great big glasses, feet too large and a cowlick.

He didn't mind. The name Poindexter, I mean. We met in the middle of the school year in eighth grade. And at the beginning of summer, when it was time for Poindexter to leave for the exchange thing, he came and sat with me on my front porch for an almost all-nighter. We kissed there on the swing. Me sitting with my legs tucked up under me, and him with his arm across the back of our shared seat.

It was my first kiss and it broke open a thought inside, one I had been sheltering for months now: Poindexter was more than a friend and I would miss him bad when he was gone. For a moment I let the thought come into my head that everybody I loved left, but that wasn't quite true. While Dad and Madelaine wouldn't be back, Mara hadn't taken a hike and neither had my mother—except emotionally—and Poindexter would return in two months. I could handle that. Maybe.

"I'll write you," he said, his breath warm on my forehead where his lips had come to rest.

Quick tears sprang to my eyes. "You better," I said. "I want you to know I am a great letter writer."

"I know you are." He meant the letters I was always writing to my father and sister.

"I don't think it's fair for you to go right now," I said.

Out in the yard fireflies painted tiny points of light that almost seemed like a memory till one flamed up again in a different place. The air was warm and busy with a rain that promised to wash through that evening, maybe even while the two of us sat on the porch. Behind me, closed away in her office, Mom worked on a research paper that was going into a university journal. I could almost hear the click of the computer keys as she worked.

"What do you mean?" Poindexter asked. "Why isn't it fair?"

Because of this feeling, I thought, but I didn't say anything, just rested my head on his shoulder and worried.

"The time will go by quicker than a flash, Carolina," Poindexter said. He talked the same way his mother did, as if he had no problems.

"Not for me," I said.

But I was wrong. Time did go by fast. Letters came from him and I wrote more than I sent because the kiss had opened floodgates and I couldn't hold in the words.

While Mom didn't ever seem to notice that something had changed in me, Mara did.

"Tell me everything, Carolina," she said the first time I saw her after Poindexter's plane had taken him across an ocean from me.

"Tell you what?" A smiled edged to my lips.

We were in Mara's room, the place I had christened the Bra Sanctuary, lying on her double bed. I sat up, looking away from my friend, through the glass doors that led from her bedroom to the outdoor pool.

"I know something's happened. I can tell by the look on your face. He kissed you, didn't he?"

Mara never waited for an answer, just broke into

peals of laughter that echoed around in my head and made me smile all the more.

"Finally," she shouted. "I bet you a hundred dollars it was the bra."

I looked back at her. "It couldn't have been. I wasn't wearing it. Just Madelaine's undershirt."

"*Just* the undershirt?" Mara's voice rose to a screech.

"I meant," I said, embarrassed by my own words, "that that was all I had under my clothes."

"Even one of Madelaine's old worn-out bits of left-over underwear could look pretty darn sexy." Mara really laughed now.

"Come on," I said, slapping at her. "You know what I meant."

Mara got a hold of herself. "Tell me all about it."

"What's there to tell? You already know everything." And about kissing and dating and guys, it's true. Mara started dating before Dad and Madelaine left.

"Did he kiss you? Did Poindexter lay lips on you?"

It was right at that moment, right when Mara said his name, that I realized I wanted to keep my time with Poindexter to myself, safe inside my heart, along with other soft thoughts and feelings.

"We talked," I said.

"He *did* kiss you," she said. And I'm not sure if she really knew or was only guessing.

"We watched fireflies," I said. And then I clamped my mouth shut because I had already said too much. Maybe now the sight of fireflies would not make my stomach flip-flop when I combined them with my memories of the swing.

I let Mara guess at everything and finally got her off the track by mentioning David, her newest heart-throb.

I held on to the memory of my best guy friend and me in that swing and wished there had been a few more good feelings like that to file away. And if I got too lonely for Poindexter, I crept from my room, when it was late and the fireflies were lighting up the night and a heavy rain waited, and sat on the front porch till dawn cleared my thoughts and I could sleep.

Chapter 3

A Note to You

I hope you don't mind me addressing this bunch-of-nothing story to you like, well, you know, like you're the reader. It's all so confusing, so lonely, to be just one. I keep thinking that by my writing this down, it will help me figure it through. Maybe clean out the sore spots of my memory and heart so that things aren't so crusted over.

A week before school started, and the evening before Poindexter came home, Mom came into my room. She had pushed her owllike glasses up onto her head so they held back her hair.

"Carolina," she said. "We need to have a little chat." Her voice was soft and low. It always reminds me of thick melted chocolate, though I'm not sure that a sound can really remind you of a taste.

"All right," I said, and closed the book I was reading. It was one of Madelaine's and a love story. Madelaine always liked love stories, especially the ones Louise Plummer wrote, because they made her laugh. At least that's what Madelaine said.

Mom sat down on the edge of my bed. "Things have got to change," she said.

I got a sick feeling in my stomach. The kind where you think you have to throw up and so you swallow a lot. "What things?"

Mom waved her hands around a bit like she was pulling in fresh air. "Us," she said.

"Us change? More than we already have?" But somehow I knew what she meant.

Mom leaned near and I could smell the fragrance of White Shoulders, cloudlike, near her face. I shut my eyes and breathed in deep.

"Yes, Carolina. You and me. Without your dad. Without Madelaine." Mom's throat sounded like it might close up tight on her. She reached for my hand, but before she could touch me I moved away.

"He didn't have to take her," I said.

Mom didn't say anything. She never does, not about that. But she looked straight at me. Her eyes were the color of an early-morning sky, so blue people thought they were fake.

"You're lucky," I remembered Madelaine saying. "To have Mom's eye color and Dad's auburn hair. And you don't have one freckle. Not one. It's not fair. I'm so mousy."

I shook my head at the memory because to me Madelaine hadn't been mousy at all. She had been a just-right older sister.

"Wait before you say no," Mom said, and I let her believe that I was saying no to her and not to my memory. It was easier that way. "It's a new school year for both of us. I'm getting some great classes to teach at the university. You're starting high school. It's all so . . ." Mom waved her hands again. "So new."

"Yeah," I said, "it is." And I believed it, that feeling of newness, especially when I thought of seeing Poindexter the next day. Maybe sitting with him in the swing on the porch. And even going to the same school, though he'd be a grade ahead. But there was still a part of me that was sad and sore and old-feeling.

Mom tried to take both my hands in hers but I wouldn't let her. She pretended not to notice. "We can never forget what's happened. And I'm not thinking we should. But we need to move on. This October it'll be a year. And I think we need to enjoy the time we have together."

I nodded because, inside, my guts were wrestling

with each other. Yes, it had been almost a year, but how long does it take to quit missing people you love? Things were changing, both Mom and I were proof of that. But I didn't really want them to change. I wanted time to be back before the trip to California that Dad and Madelaine took, I wanted time to be pre-bra days, I wanted time to be back before there was so much to worry about.

"I think we can, kind of, you know, start over."

"I can try," I said.

Mom let out a sigh like maybe she had been holding her breath waiting for my answer.

"I'm not sitting around anymore," she said. "I'm going to start living again. And I'm planning on being a part of your life again too, if you'll let me. Meals together. I'll help with your homework—if you need it. Maybe even a little trip. We could drive up to St. Augustine."

I nodded, a lump coming into my throat, though I wasn't too sure why.

"And there's always Garret," Mom said, smiling. I felt surprise spread throughout me, tingling all the way to my fingertips.

"What do you mean?"

"I noticed changes in him. And in you."

"What kind of changes?" Had she seen us that night, so long ago, on the swing? Had she, oh please no, seen us *kiss*? My face went red at the possibility.

"I never said anything because I was still feeling bad." Mom looked across the room, like maybe, for a moment, she had forgotten I was there. Then she looked back at me and smiled a sad sort of smile. "First love is so sweet," she said, getting to her feet. "Can you hardly wait to see him again? I wonder how much he's changed."

I shrugged, not quite ready to let Mom into that part of my life. But my stomach flipped at the thought of meeting Poindexter again. "Probably he's still the same Garret," I said, and the words seemed empty.

"You don't have to tell me anything, honey," Mom said, and she walked out of the room, talking as she went. "But I'll be here, from now on. No more absentee mother. It's bad enough missing a husband and a child." She glanced at me. "A father and a sister."

She turned again and I watched my mother leave, her steps slow and deliberate, and even though I wanted to call her back I didn't. I sat still on my bed and toyed with thoughts, the ones Mom had brought up. About her being around from now on. I even touched the tip of the idea of her missing a husband and a daughter. But mostly I thought about the easiest thing—that Poindexter might have changed.

And I wasn't so sure I liked that at all.

———

It was just a trip, nothing to worry about. Dad had asked us both—me and Madelaine—to go. I felt like I should stay with Mom, who was working and couldn't get off from classes. And anyway, I've always hated flying. They were on their way home at least, I found a little comfort in that. That they had been together and that maybe California had been fun.

Sometimes, when my mind seems empty, I suddenly find it full of remembrances of my father, traveling around the world for his company and my sister so young, thinking she was mousy. I think about them together those last few minutes. Did they hold hands? Did they have time to? Were they afraid?

That's what bothers me the most, wondering about them being afraid, because the thought of a falling plane terrifies me.

Chapter

4

My bedroom is on the side of the house that faces
Poindexter's home. I'm up on the second floor,
in a small corner room that's painted a creamy yellow.
I've always liked this room and I wish Madelaine
could have been in here. Kind of blessed it with her
presence. I know that sounds dumb, but that's the
kind of sister she was. Not holy or religious, that's not
what I mean. And even though I remember her perfect, she wasn't. We screamed and fought with each
other sometimes. She fought with Mom and Dad. I
wore her clothes and she hated it. She came in my
room and I hated that. Mostly, though, we got along.

But that's not what I was talking about. I was talking about this bedroom.

I sat in my room and from where I leaned on the windowsill I could see Poindexter's house and driveway. I was reading, sort of, with one eye, and watching with the other. Really I waited for him to come home.

I'm not sure what it was that I expected. But it seemed if I was able to sit there at my window, watching everything that happened, it might mean this new school year would be good. That my heart wouldn't ache so much and, maybe, time with Poindexter would be a little like it had been the night before he left and still more, if you know what I mean.

Around three-thirty the phone rang, but I didn't move even though I have an extension in my room. Mom called up from downstairs that it was Mara. I set my book down and pulled the phone as close to the window as I could manage, but I wasn't quite able to see Poindexter's driveway anymore. The privet hedge was in the way.

"Carolina," Mara said. "Is he home yet?"

"Is who home?" Sometimes I wonder if Mara has some kind of crystal ball that lets her look into my life.

Mara laughed. "Is Poindexter home? I thought today was *the* day."

"Hmm," I said, trying to fake it that I hadn't had this very day marked on my calendar, and my heart, since weeks before he had left. "You might be right."

"Well, is he back?"

"How should I know?" And I meant that. I could no longer see the driveway. For all I knew, he was coming home at this very second and I was going to miss everything.

"You mean you're not watching from your window? You have a perfect view from your window."

"I do?" I asked, straining to see past the sheer curtains, stretching out on one leg, trying to peer through the glass and listen to Mara at the same time.

"Do you think he's changed?"

"Actually, I hadn't given it much thought," I said. A lie. A big lie. I was worried sick Poindexter had changed. There were too many changes in my life. I needed something settled. Something pure and the same as it had always been. I needed Poindexter. All of a sudden tears threatened. I blinked my eyes quick.

"*I've* thought about it," Mara said, "and *I'm* not in love with him the way you are. That means you've *had* to have been wondering about him."

"Neither am I," I said. "In love I mean."

I heard the car then, and caught a glimpse of the dark green top moving down the drive. I could barely get out the words, "Could you hold on a second, please, Mara?"

I didn't wait for her to answer but set the phone on my bedside table and leapt across my bed, catapulting myself right next to the window and almost slamming myself into the glass, just as the car passed. I saw Poindexter, sitting on this side of the Wagoneer, saw as he waved to me. I was so horrified that I couldn't lift my hand in response. I hid next to the wall, then a second later allowed myself to peer out at the taillights. My heart pounded.

I sucked in a deep breath. *Why, he's been watching for me.* I was sure of it. He had been looking up at my window.

I touched my hair, which was pulled back in a barrette, felt where some of it had fallen loose past my shoulders.

When would we talk?

I sat on the edge of my bed, then fell back, a small scream escaping my lips. "He's home," I said to the ceiling. I wiped my sweating palms on a pillow that decorated my bed. "He's home."

I couldn't believe the feeling of excitement. "Calm down, now."

With a deep breath, I sat up. I made my way to the window the long way, so that if he was looking up at me he wouldn't see me looking down at him.

But the driveway was empty, the garage door closed. There was no Poindexter for me to gawk at.

I stood, silent, at my window and rested my forehead on the pane of glass.

It was then that I remembered Mara. I ran to the phone.

"Are you there?" I asked.

"Barely," she said. And then, "He's home now, isn't he?"

How could she know? Was it in my voice? That thrill of having seen his hand wave at me, was it somehow seeping out through my pores and traveling down the line to Mara only a mile away? How did she always know these kinds of things?

"Are you still thinking about him?" I asked. "Why, I bet he's in your thoughts more than he's in mine." That couldn't be possible.

Mara gave a little giggle. "I have my own man," she said.

And I lay down on the bed so we could talk about nothing now that the most important moment of summer had happened with the arrival of the deep green car from the airport.

❦ ❦ ❦

A Note to You

Maybe I was putting too much into what might happen with Garret, the boy next door, my friend nicknamed Poindexter. Maybe I was expecting too much from a kiss and an evening two months before. But I was going to see, and let these feelings be a salve for my heart and scratched-up soul.

Chapter 5

Poindexter came over after dinner.

"Hey," he said when I opened the door.

"Hey," I said, but that any word came out at all was a miracle.

"How's it going?"

I kind of nodded my head and at that moment, it seemed, my tongue swelled up in my mouth till it felt like it was the size of our high-school football stadium.

Poindexter made an awkward move, his hand reaching for the doorjamb. Maybe he knew about my tongue and felt like he had been cast in a horror movie—*The Tongue Next Door.*

"You've changed," I managed to say.

"What?" As he reached for the door again, his hand touched my wrist. An electric current seemed to run through my body, shocking my tongue back to normal.

"Come on in." I opened the screen door wide.

Poindexter smiled, a smile that seemed brighter than it ever had before. "All right." He followed me into the house.

We went into the living room. Our sofa is the same one we had before Dad and Madelaine left. Mom had only been able to lose some of our memories. The patterns on the sofa, she said, reminded her too much of Dad and his love for color. Splashes of color, almost like from a painter's palette, covered the material. She couldn't bear to sell it or give it away.

We sat down together, and the sofa breathed out a touch of air like maybe it had been watching us at the doorway and was glad Poindexter was inside too.

I looked at him. Poindexter *had* changed. Just like Mom and Mara had said he might. He was, well, bigger. Thinner, a little. His eyes seemed larger and browner than I remembered. And his hair was wavy. It didn't even stick up anymore. How could I call him Poindexter if his hair didn't do what it had done not that long ago? And how in the world could a person change so fast in a couple of months?

"You look nice, Carolina," he said, and he took hold of my fingers.

I touched my hair with my other hand. Then I

checked my face for any leftover dinner. Mom and I had eaten a spinach salad. I felt sure something green and leafy was wrapped around a front tooth.

"You've gotten . . . older," I said, making sure I kept my top lip low and unmoving. "Or something."

"We did a lot of bike riding."

I nodded. *It did you good,* I thought, but I didn't say anything. *Not that you were bad before,* my mind corrected; then it raced to that last evening together, an evening made perfect in my memory. My tongue went over my teeth in little scrubbing motions.

"Thanks for all the letters."

I nodded again. "I didn't send you everything."

Poindexter's, I mean Garret's, eyebrows went up. "How come?"

I wanted to grin at him and almost did. My cheeks turned pink at the thought of leftover dinner waiting to be displayed. "Too many. You know how I like to write. Anyway, I wanted you to have something to do other than just read stuff from home."

A Note to You

Upstairs, tucked away in my room, are three envelopes fat with letters. One marked "Poindexter," one marked "Daddy" and the third with Madelaine's name on it. There just used to be the two. And of course, before the leaving, none at all. I've filled these envelopes with my thoughts and hurts and the few happy times I seem to have.

"Did you save them?" Garret asked. He shifted around a little till he sat closer to me. Our knees, bare because we both wore shorts, almost touched.

"Yeah," I said. "I don't know if they're for you to read. They might be too . . . you know." I waved my hand, the one that was free from Garret, around in the air. It was like I was clearing the way for the words that were at the front of my brain. *They were too personal, too much to send after just one kiss.* I let the thought and the sentence drop.

Garret looked back, his face serious. "Let's go for a walk. You want to?"

"Yeah," I said. "Let me tell Mom." It was an excuse to check for leftover dinner. I walked out of the room fast and into the dining room, where a mirror hung above a sideboard of dishes my great-grandmother had owned. Mom waited around the corner.

"Whoah!" I said, surprised to find her there.

Mom's face turned red. "I'm sorry," she said, her voice a whisper. "I was listening in."

My mouth dropped open. I didn't care if *she* saw spinach. "Mom. Spying?"

"I'm sorry, Carolina. I don't know what made me do it."

"Mom."

"I've just missed so much of your life lately."

"So you thought you should fill yourself in by becoming a part-time detective?"

"Shhh," Mom said, holding her finger to her lips. "I don't want Poindexter to know."

I rolled my eyes and made my way to the mirror. I checked my teeth. Clean. Phew.

"So can we go?" I whispered.

"Of course." Mom grinned, a big grin, a spinach-free grin. I wondered if she ever worried about her teeth.

We walked out to the living room. Garret stood near the fireplace. The inside was clean because Dad hadn't been here to make fires and because it was summer.

"Mrs. McKinney, your daughter looked a lot like you. And a little like you, too, Carolina." Garret held a photograph, a picture of Dad and me and Madelaine, all on the beach.

Mom gasped in air. "Oh," she said, and I knew she felt like she'd been gut-punched. I could tell by the look in her eyes. I'd seen that very look on my own face when I was surprised again that neither Dad nor Madelaine was coming home.

Garret put the picture down. "Sorry," he said. "I didn't mean—"

"Oh, no." Mom interrupted him. "You're fine. Really."

I was caught in the awkwardness of the situation. Caught in the pain of missing my sister and my father.

"Dad usually took the pictures," I said, and my voice sounded fake to me. "We were down by the jetty, remember, Mom, and you told Dad you'd take the shot."

Mom nodded but she was looking away, staring off to another day, I think.

"That's why the picture's a little blurry," I said. I spoke fast, trying to cover up for mine and Mom's pain and the embarrassment Garret had to be feeling. "Mom's still not that good of a photographer."

That was the truth. I don't think we'd even unpacked any of Dad's gear since the move. I know we hadn't taken any pictures, not of me, not of the two of us.

We all stood in the living room, stood there by the fireplace, Garret with his red face, me trying to patch things up with third-grade words and Mom looking at everything except us.

"Let's go," I said at last. The words released us all from the painful spell.

"Yeah, right," Garret said. "Let's go." His voice was soft. "Umm, see you, Mrs. McKinney."

Mom didn't answer.

———

The thing is, Garret is right. About Madelaine looking so much like Mom. Of course, my sister couldn't know how great she looked. I think that's a law or something, not to realize how good you've got something. At least that's the way it is with me. Anyway, that was the last picture taken of Madelaine, and she never got to see it, never got to see that with her growing up she looked a lot like Mom.

The memory is so clear—us driving out that morning. It was windy, but the light, Dad said, was good. So when the wind died down a bit, Mom snapped off a few shots. I've hidden the others in my room. Some days, when I am especially lonely for my sister, I pull the pictures out from their hiding place on the top shelf of my closet and look at them. I smooth my fingers over the faces of my father and sister. And if I concentrate, I can almost hear her laugh, almost hear her arguing with me. Almost.

Madelaine wouldn't have liked these pictures as well as the one on the mantel. She would say her hair is too messy, or her eyes weren't open wide enough. But when I look at these that's not what I see at all.

And to think she thought she was mousy.

Chapter 6

Garret was quiet the whole walk. And we were out late, too. Until the coming night made the air look gray.

My street dead-ends right into a horse pasture. Garret and I stopped here. Trees edged up along the fence. A few horses, not yet in for the evening, trotted over to where we stood. Their thick smell, oatsy and full, came over toward me on a soft breeze, a breeze not strong enough to drive away the mosquitoes.

"Boy, I screwed that up royal," Garret said.

I wasn't sure what to say. Overhead the streetlamp buzzed and threw down an orange glow. I bent over to pick some cheat grass. It came up with a squeak. A horse, one with a dark muzzle, leaned near and I fed him the long, rough grass. I had to think of an answer.

"No, you didn't," I said at last.

"Did you see her face?"

I nodded. Garret moved up behind me and picked some grass too. He fed a horse that had a white splotch on its forehead.

"We don't ever talk about it," I said.

"You and your mom?"

"Yeah." A funny thing happened then. Right at that very moment I wanted to share everything there was about Madelaine and Dad with Garret. I wanted to tell him about the home videos I'd seen Mom watching really late at night. Videos of all of us, before. The ones I sometimes crouched in the hallway to watch, way back in the shadows so Mom wouldn't know I was there. I wanted to tell him about how sometimes, when I was scared, I could go into Madelaine's room in the middle of the night and climb into her bed. "Scrooch up close, Carolina," she'd whisper. I could almost hear her voice right there in the dark, by the horses, with Garret.

I heard a bike come up then, the sound of the tires on the street, and when I turned around Mara was there.

"Mr. Poindexter!" she shouted.

Garret turned around. "Hey, Mara."

"Carolina." Mara said this like we hadn't just spoken that very afternoon, like maybe she had been missing *me* or something. "Have you gotten your class schedule yet?"

"You know I have," I said, but she didn't wait for my answer. She had diarrhea of the mouth, like she does sometimes.

"The extracurricular activities."

"What?" Garret asked.

Mara threw her bike onto the road and ran to hug him hello. The back tire spun on and on, making a *whir* sound. She wrapped her arms around his neck.

"We've got to take one of those classes together," she said, looking up at him, her long hair appearing longer because of the way she held her head.

"What are you talking about, Mara?" I came up to where she still held on to Garret.

"School. Classes." Mara moved away from Garret, who gaped at her. "We get to choose. Not like last year where they *said* we got to choose. This is the real thing. I have a schedule of classes."

"That came a month ago," I said. "I've signed up for everything I wanted." It hadn't been easy. I kept wondering what Madelaine had taken in high school her first and only year. I should have listened to her more.

"Me too," Garret said. "I went over it this afternoon."

Mara slapped her hand at me. "I know, silly. But we haven't all been together till right this very minute."

I rolled my eyes sideways and planted my hands on my hips. "You're right about that."

A Note to You

I know I know I know I know I know. You warned me plenty of times that I should watch my back. I think she knew you didn't like her so much. Here's what I want to know: How could you know years ahead about what would happen and me not have a clue? I thought I was the one living it. Well, maybe only partway.

A horse blew out a breath of air to remind us we should be paying attention to him.

"If we don't sign up right now, together, you know, find that *one* special class . . ." Mara reached into her back pocket and pulled out a light blue booklet that had a schedule of classes we could choose from. She clutched it to her chest, closed her eyes and said, "High school is going to be such a blast. It's going to be wonderful." The words came out like she was praying to the gods of academia.

Garret laughed.

Mara's eyes snapped open. She raised the booklet to slap him and he moved behind me, gripping my shoulders in his warm hands. He pulled me back till I was right against his body. He was a lot taller than me, so much taller that his chin came close to my left eye as he peered toward Mara. It all happened so fast that I forgot to breathe.

"We can choose school tomorrow," he said. "I don't want to think about that kind of prison sentence at this moment." His arms were around my waist now and his words were loud in my ear. His face rested against mine and I could smell spearmint on his breath.

"Fine," Mara said, and she gave me an evil grin. "Carolina, I'm leaving my schedule with *you* so *you* can look through it. We'll want to be in at least one class together, won't we? Whatever you do, do not let Poindexter here see what *I've* chosen. *He's* not allowed."

She laughed again, a happy laugh, and picked up her bicycle. "Glad you're back," she said.

"Yeah, see ya."

"Bye, Carolina." Mara was on the bike now, ready to pedal away.

"I'll call you tomorrow with the extracurricular class I'd like," I said.

I didn't want to move from Garret's arms. I hadn't felt this comfortable in such a long time. So long.

And yet I felt embarrassed to be wrapped up like this in front of my best girlfriend.

"You better call me," Mara said, and now the laugh was in her voice, though her face looked serious.

I felt weird. A way I'd never felt about Mara before. Jealous almost.

"She'll call you," Garret said.

"I'll call you," I said, and my voice was almost a whisper.

Mara pedaled away.

I expected to be released then, for Garret to let me go from his warm, comforting arms, but that didn't happen. Instead he held on. "Carolina," he said. "Carolina."

His lips touched my hair, touched my face near my ear, touched next to my nose.

I turned toward Garret and breathed in deep the smell of him.

After Garret walked me home, I climbed into bed and watched the patterns of leaf shadows play on the ceiling. Tears filled my eyes, hot, guilty tears that seemed to burn the back of my throat.

"Madelaine," I whispered.

Chapter 7

We decided on photography because I had all Dad's old equipment and Garret was interested in darkroom techniques. Mara was just interested in us sticking together.

Those few days before school I was surprised how much time she spent with Garret and me. And she stopped calling him Poindexter too.

The evenings were mine and his, though. Sometimes he came over for a meal, and sometimes I visited at his house. And of course we had slow walks and hours on my front porch swing.

The funny thing is, the jealousy I felt at seeing Mara on Garret's first night home continued every time the three of us were together. The feeling was foreign and I couldn't quite figure it out. When she showed up it was like I developed an instant bad taste on my tongue that I couldn't get rid of. Even when it was just her and me.

The night before school started, Garret and I went walking, just the two of us. Hand in hand we made our way around the horse field to a secluded driveway that ran nearly a mile to the owner's huge house.

The driveway was shaded with magnificent oaks. The tire tracks were cobblestone, and groomed grass grew down the middle. Wildflowers grew along the edges, spilling over the sides, like they wanted the chance to run free. Spanish moss hung low out of some of the trees, so low that I could have touched it if I'd wanted to. The lane was a private drive, but Garret and I crossed over the white rail fence to walk there anyway.

"I love this place," he said in a low voice, holding my hand and helping me over a fence I could have vaulted.

"I do too." My words were lame but exactly what I felt. *There's no Mara here,* I thought, but I didn't say it. After all, she was my best girlfriend.

"We're alone."

I nodded.

A Note to You

Garret and I kissed, yes. Don't get me wrong, I loved the kissing part. But that wasn't all. He talked to me. He held my hand. And he listened to my heart: to the fact that Mom was edging her way into my life like the wildflowers trying to edge into the driveway and I wasn't sure about it; to the fact that I was nervous about this first year of high school; to the fact that I just felt all alone. I didn't tell him about the guilt, though, that I felt deep in my heart. It happened when the good times with him became too sweet. I wondered if Mom felt it too, this guilt mixed in with a heavy dose of grief, from missing our family.

We walked down the driveway, hand in hand, each staying on our cobblestone tire track. The night pressed in on us, heavy and expectant, the air pregnant with rain. The sweet smell of magnolias floated in the air. Mosquitoes buzzed. All around us fireflies lit up the evening.

Why me? I thought. My stomach and insides flip-flopped with a sudden happiness. *How did I get so lucky to be with Garret?*

"School tomorrow," I told him. "I'm gonna hate that."

He pulled my hand to his lips and kissed it. It was my right hand and he kissed between the second and third knuckles, making my heart explode with what felt like Painted Lady butterflies.

"You're going to be okay. It'll be fun. I know the school. I can show you around."

"You are the expert, Mr. Sophomore." I paused. "It's scary, though. College-prep classes. Shorter lunches." I took in a deep breath at the thought.

"We can sit together in photography, if we all get that class." Garret pulled me so that I bumped into him a little.

We had reached the end of the driveway now, or at least as far as we ever went when we crossed the No Trespassing sign, the imaginary line we had drawn ourselves that said *No farther than this.* From here I could see the house, huge and beautiful, nestled in among hundreds of trees. Past that were the horse stables, and then the pasture that butted into my dead-end street.

I stood quiet, looking at the redbrick home with the white columns in front.

"I love that house," Garret said.

"Yeah?" I was surprised.

"I want to buy it. For you. And me."

"What?"

"After school. After college. When I get a good job. I want to come back here, climb over the fence like you and I do, and see if they won't sell us this place."

Garret looked at me then in the deepening dusk. "Carolina," he said, "I really like you. I mean, I really like you."

I nodded because I didn't quite trust my voice not to give me away. *I'm past like, Garret. I've fallen into the love thing,* I wanted to say, but I said nothing, just kept nodding until he put his forehead on my forehead.

Down below, a garage door started to open.

"Ack," I said.

"Run," Garret said. He spun me around until I faced up the driveway and he started sprinting, dragging me along behind him. And uphill, too.

"Oh no, oh no," I said. Adrenaline pumped through my veins, making me run faster than I ever had before.

"They're coming, we're gonna get caught," Garret said, and somehow he burst forward, nearly tugging my arm right out of its socket.

"Wait," I wanted to say, but only a grunt came out. I was running far too fast for my own legs. I fell on one knee.

Garret looked behind us once. "Eep," he said. He jerked me sideways and I skidded over the hump in the driveway, through the wildflowers and into the woods.

A few moments later a car came up the driveway.

I expected someone to holler, "We've seen you kids, come on out, we've already called the cops," but the car just passed.

"Carolina, are you okay?" Garret knelt in front of me and cradled my face in his hands. Behind him were the fireflies, fluorescent almost, coming and going.

I nodded. "Yeah," I managed to say. My heart pounded so hard I could feel it in my throat. I had to breathe through my mouth to get enough air.

"Wow," Garret said. "That was not cool."

I looked sideways at him. "I'll say," I said, and then I threw back my head and laughed.

"Shhh," he said.

I couldn't tell if he was smiling or not. It was too dark now, here in the trees and with it being so late, with only fireflies to blink in the night air.

I fell back in the grass and flowers and fallen leaves and screeched with laughter.

"Shhh, Carolina, we're still not out of danger. We're still on private property."

"I'm sorry," I said, laughing so that I could barely get the words out of my mouth. "I'm sorry. You're just so right. That *wasn't* cool." I rolled to one side, clutching my stomach, laughing so loud that I was sure the people in the car would back up to where we were hidden, this time bringing the police with them. But I couldn't stop myself.

The laughter overcame me and I was crying. Crying and laughing at the same time.

"What?" Garret asked. "Carolina, what?"

Tears took over laughter and I sobbed now. I'd crossed the threshold somehow and I couldn't get back. I covered my face with my arms, tried to roll over in the leaves and bury my sudden sorrow. But Garret pulled me up and I rested against him.

"I was just so scared," I said, needing an answer, needing to excuse myself.

Garret said nothing.

"My knee hurts," I said. But really it was my heart. I'd been so afraid. But there were worse things. Worse fears. What about Dad? And what about Madelaine? How had they felt falling all that way?

Dear God, help me, I prayed in my head and heart. *I can't think of this.*

After a few minutes, I got to my feet. There were leaves in my hair and my nose was stuffed up and I wasn't even sure my knee would bend.

Garret wrapped an arm around me, and I walked up the driveway exhausted from the experience and my thoughts.

And there was Mara waiting for us, under a streetlight, glowing orange in her beauty.

"You're bleeding, Carolina," she said.

It's funny how this sadness is. Sometimes it's thin and strong like you're wrapped in heavy-duty plastic wrap. Sometimes it's thick and pounding like when something's in your throat and you're not sure it's gonna come out. It's guilt and heartache and missing people all lumped together. And I hate it. I really do.

Chapter 8

"What are you doing here, Mara?" Garret asked. He stood at the fence, helping me now because he had to. My knee hurt. So did my heart. In fact my heart was more crippling than my knee.

"I'm glad to see you, too, Garret," Mara said. She stuck her tongue out at him. "What happened to you, woman?" Mara moved close and reached out. I took her hands and she helped me down from the fence in the front while Garret held on to me at the back.

"I shouldn't have worn shorts," I said. "Now I get to start high school with a scab." *Great,* I thought. *I said* scab *in front of Garret. I'm a Poindexter.*

"Can you hardly wait?" Mara said when I stood safely next to her. She folded her hands prayer fashion.

"Tomorrow school starts. We get to see if we can get into photography together."

Already I knew I wasn't in any of Mara's classes and that I shared English with Garret. That's what happens when your mother is an English professor like mine. You get moved ahead. He had two classes with Mara, though, algebra and French, because any grade could take those. That thought made the bad taste come into my mouth so that I wanted to spit good.

I didn't say anything, just tested my knee and began to hobble toward home.

"We need to go early," Mara said, and she moved from my side to Garret's.

In the distance, lightning played out over the ocean, sectioning off the purple sky.

"If we're there first thing, the three of us can see about adding photography. What do you say, Garret?" We were under another light now. I saw Mara reach for him. She touched the sleeve of his shirt, then ran her hand down his arm.

"Not too early," I said. And what I meant was, *Mara, move your hand.*

"Yeah," said Garret. "I agree with Carolina. Not too early."

"But we might miss the class." Mara's voice was whiny sounding. "Then we won't be together. The three of us."

Shut up, I thought.

"We'll swing it somehow," Garret said. And he turned his attention to me. "Carolina, are you all right? Can you make it home?"

"Sure," I said. My hands started shaking with relief. It washed over my hot skin, cooling it. Garret liked me, even with beautiful Mara right there, picking at his sleeve. He liked *me*.

"That's a real road rash," he said.

"Yeah, it looks like it hurts," Mara said.

"It stings," I said.

"Doesn't that look like it hurts, Garret?" she said.

He nodded. "We're almost home, Carolina."

Too bad, I thought, but what I said was, "Almost."

"I could stay with you tonight, if you wanted," Mara said.

A funny feeling ran through me, a feeling the opposite of relief. It made my skin prickle and turn warmer. "It's a school night," I said.

Mara laughed. "We're in high school now, dummy."

"Yeah," I said, my mind racing for an excuse. "But I think Mom will want me alone."

"Whatever," Mara said, and she sounded insulted.

But I didn't care. This growing yuckiness was filling up my soul. I knew now why she wanted to be in the class with Garret and me and I didn't really think I had the energy for it. *I can't fight you and win, Mara,* I thought.

We were silent the rest of the way home, but the night was full of sounds. Frogs crying for rain. Crickets singing. Even an owl called once.

Thunder rumbled in the distance and a breeze rushed in from the ocean. With it came a misty rain and a salty smell that reminded me of my own tears.

Mom sat waiting for me on the front porch. Even before I was on our property she was at my side, leaping down the steps and running, barefoot, through the lawn.

"What happened?" she asked.

"I just skinned my knee," I said.

"Let me take care of it," she said, and hustled me off.

"See you tomorrow," Garret called. "I'll pick you up. We can go together."

"Me too," Mara said. "I'll stop by too."

I turned to wave from the porch. Mara stood close to Garret, holding him by the elbow. Her voice carried over to me. "Walk me home, why don't you?" she said.

"It's late," Garret said. "See ya." He took off across my front yard and pushed through the privet hedge to his house.

"Well," said Mom, and she moved me inside, directing me by the shoulders.

In the bathroom, Mom took out all her medicinal supplies and doctored my knee. I sat on the floor leaning against the side of the tub, my eyes closed, feeling her cool hands as she gently cleansed my wound. This was as close as I could get to her.

"Look at this," she said. "Dirt *and* grass. How did you manage it?"

I shrugged. How long had it been since Mom had touched me in a *let me take care of you* way? I couldn't remember. Certainly not since the crash.

"School tomorrow," she said, her voice as soothing as her touch. "What are you wearing?"

"Clothes," I said. I opened an eye and looked at her. Her head was close to mine. So close I could see gray hairs.

"Mom!" I said, a gasp pulling out of my throat. "When?"

"What?" Her hands jerked. "Don't scare me like that. Did I hurt you?"

"No." I was surprised to feel my hands shaking.

"What then?"

"Nothing," I said. Maybe she didn't know. Maybe she had missed the gray. I had. How? How had I missed that, my mother getting older?

"You need to be more careful, Carolina," Mom said. Her head was still tipped down almost as if she were bowing. I wanted to put my hands in her graying hair and do something to change things back to the way they had been. How long? How long would this last? "You need to be more careful."

"I will."

She smoothed the extra-fat Band-Aid over the scrape. Her tapered nails were perfectly polished, I noticed.

"No, I mean about Mara."

My stomach gave a squeeze.

"What?"

Mom avoided my eyes. "Nothing really," she said. "I just want you to be careful. She seems . . ."

I stood. Now she looked up at me from the floor.

"Maybe I'm imagining it," she said.

"She likes him," I said. "I know. I've seen the way she looks at him too." I felt like I was in a bad movie where all the lines had been said before in a thousand other bad movies.

Mom went to hug me to her, and I wanted her to— at least a small part of me did. But I couldn't let her. When she came close I put my hand out to stop her. She grabbed my hand and squeezed it with both of hers, like she was hugging me in a strange way. I closed my eyes a moment and in my head, she was fine again. And so was I.

I thought of my mother, not even thirty-six, while I was in bed that night. I made a tent over my knees and wondered. What had Dad's and Madelaine's leaving done to her? Taken her peace, like it had mine? And now her hair was gray. What else?

Chapter
9

The next morning I got up early because I couldn't sleep. In the predawn light, I stood in my nightgown and gazed out the window toward Garret's house. A gentle breeze pushed in through the screen, making the curtains move a little. The air was sweet-smelling. What was Garret doing right now?

Mara's face came to mind. What was *she* doing? Planning something for the day? Maybe to take my spot in any *special* class the three of us were in together?

I shook my head. "Stop it," I said to myself. "Mara is your friend."

I went to the bathroom, hoping to talk myself out of my Mara mood. I climbed into the tub, leaving my bad knee outside the flowered curtain. Showering that way wasn't easy to do.

I talked to Madelaine.

"All right," I said. Hot water poured down on my head, running into my eyes, soothing me almost back to sleep. "You were supposed to have done this with me, so I wouldn't have to go alone. Madelaine, you were supposed to have helped me through it all."

I washed down with a fragrant soap.

"I want you to know I think this is a dirty trick. I'd have rather followed you around a lot, gotten compared to you 'cause you were such a good student." Madelaine had only been a fair student, though. There were other things that were more important to her, but I couldn't think of anything at the moment. Not even a year and I was forgetting. Why couldn't the pain go with the memory?

I hopped around one-legged until my bad knee was in the shower, then covered it with a hand towel.

"Stupid," I said under my breath. I had to stop talking to my sister. This wasn't any good. What would Mom think? I wondered if she talked this way to Dad.

I washed my hair. I could feel the towel around my knee getting wet, warming up with hot water.

In the movies, I thought, *the dead person always appears to the leftover living person.* Always. Like in that one old show *Sleepless in Seattle.* The guy's wife comes back after she dies from cancer, and visits. It happens all the time in the movies.

Just not in real life.

I sighed, cut off the water, then got out of the shower and stood dripping on the cream-colored bath mat.

I tried to look at myself in the steamy mirror. With my towel I wiped away some of the moisture. Hmmm. Things looked normal on me. Water trickled from my hair. I had breasts. Not Mara-sized breasts, but that was okay. Maybe I would grow some. And then there was the huge bandage on my knee.

"That'll set me apart," I said to my reflection.

I decided to wear 501's to cover my knee. And an old shirt of Madelaine's for luck and comfort.

Classes were classes. My English teacher was okay, a little bald man from England who had worked at Mom's university but had come over to the high school for a while so he could remember what it was like to be a kid and maybe write a young adult novel. At least that's what he said.

Garret and I sat next to each other and I wished for him to be in all my classes. I stared at him when he wasn't looking. I wanted to reach across the aisle and hold his hand, maybe kiss him. He looked so good to me. So clean and sweet-smelling and, I don't know, perfect.

"We're going to chat and read and write," I heard the teacher say. Dr. Morris from England.

"I'm a poet. I like reading poetry. But you can write whatever you want."

How about I love Garret Harrison *in different-colored inks?* I thought.

"I don't expect perfection," Dr. Morris was saying.

"That's good," somebody in the back said.

He smiled, showing yellowed, crooked teeth. "But I do expect your best. Writing can free you, if you let it." His accent was rich and soothing, thick like butter.

I love Garret I love Garret I love Garret.

"We'll pretend to use this text." Dr. Morris held up an English book. "But mostly we'll study from here." He tapped at his head. "And here." He tapped at his heart.

Garret caught me after class. "What's next, Carolina?" He grabbed my hand and gave it a squeeze. "I'll take you there. Make sure you don't get lost." He leaned forward and pressed his face close to mine.

"Thanks," I said. Mom hadn't been able to make it to the high-school introduction day. And I hadn't wanted to come alone, sorting out where my classes would be. "Chemistry. Room two-thirty, corridor A."

"Right this way," Garret said, and he pulled me through the hall, crammed with people, like he had pulled me up the driveway, only slower.

"How's your knee?"

"It's all right," I said. It was stiff and swollen. "I'm gonna live. If I make it through today."

Garret laughed. "You will," he said.

The school seemed a maze of carpeted twists and turns lined with lockered walls.

At last we got to my class, a room set up with tall tables and what looked something like the bar stools at my house.

"I gotta run," Garret said. "I've got to get back to algebra."

"You don't want to be late," I said. My stomach jumped at the thought of his leaving me alone. *Stay with me, Garret,* I thought. *Stay with me all day. I'm scared. Madelaine, I need you.*

"Carolina," Garret said, smiling. "You're going to be okay. Once you get used to this prison system, you'll be okay. My brothers all made it."

How did he know? "Yeah," I said.

But I had more on my mind than just school.

There was the thought that I was kind of cutting through territory that someone else should have done for me. Madelaine should have left a path for me to follow.

There was the thought of Mom, up early that morning, following me around to see that I made it okay, skinned knee and all.

Then there was the thought of Garret and Mara when I just wanted there to be Garret.

What's wrong with me? I thought later in Spanish class. *What's wrong?*

A battle raged in my head and Mara was my opponent. Did she know? Was I making everything up?

At last school swept into my brain to take over. What was that word again and why, why, why did I sign up for a language? Things were moving so fast I didn't have a chance to worry about what I couldn't quite figure out.

And Garret was right. Everything worked out.

Not only that, the three of us also got into the photography class.

Mom always used to say, Give people the benefit of the doubt. I remember her talking to Dad. "Steven," she'd say when Dad would jump to conclusions about something, "give him the benefit of the doubt." Or "You always decide the end of the story before you read the beginning and the middle." Or "Lighten up, they're just kids."

She sure as heck wasn't saying *that* to me. In fact remembering her words scared me. "You need to be more careful." It almost seemed like a premonition. Could she see the end of my story when she had been absent from the beginning and was just stepping in at the middle?

Chapter 10

"**M**om?"

"Back here, Carolina." Mom was in her office. Writing. Again.

I went to the doorway and stood looking in, leaning on the jamb.

Mom squinted up at me. Her hair was ratty. I could see she'd been pulling at her bangs, straightening the curl from them the way she does when she's nervous. I guess this newest bunch of research was giving her fits.

"Remember I told you I was thinking about taking a photography class?"

Mom straightened her arms out, twisting a little in the chair, stretching.

"No, honey," she said. "I don't."

I rolled my eyes, feeling aggravated with her all of a sudden. "Come on, Mom. I told you Garret, Mara and me were going to sign up for one of the extra things. We're gonna stick together. Remember?"

Mom shook her head. "I don't remember that, Carolina."

A Note to You

Mom and I sometimes don't speak. Okay, lots of times. We used to, before. Now, when we do talk, the words and feelings are thin and distant, like "Pass the ketchup, please," Or "I'll do the dishes tonight." In the movies when something bad happens people get closer. But not us. Mom and I have stretched out in two separate, lonely directions. So maybe I had told her about photography, maybe I hadn't.

"Jeez," I said, a little under my breath, but still loud enough that I knew Mom could hear.

"Carolina." Mom's voice was so tired that I almost felt bad. "What is it that you need?"

I softened a bit.

"Dad's camera equipment." I couldn't look Mom in the eye, so I stared over the top of her head.

"That's in the attic. Want me to help?" Mom started to get up from her desk.

"No," I said. "I can manage."

"The boxes are marked," she said.

And she was right. The attic was practically indexed, it was so neat. Mom had things stored alphabetically so once I located the "C" stack it didn't take me long at all. I found Dad's camera equipment tucked away between "Baby Things" and "Madelaine's Cat Collection." Madelaine's cats. So this was where they were. . . .

I sat down on the floor, only a little dusty, and pulled out three boxes marked "Steven's Camera Things." The room was hotter than fire and by the time I had gotten the lid off the first container sweat was rolling from my face and down my back. My hands were clammy and I felt sticky all over.

"All right," I said to myself in a whisper. "Let's see what there is." Then I started pulling things out.

Books. All kinds of books on photography. Lots by Kodak. I don't know how many on darkroom technique, though I thought of Garret when I saw those. The 35-mm handbook. The 6x7 handbook. Famous photographs, shooting in the wild, night photography. I hadn't known anyone could have been so interested in camera books. But Dad had been. His signature in the front of each manual showed me that. "This book belongs to Steven J. McKinney."

A lump came into my throat. "Don't think about it," I said.

I pulled open the second box. My hair hung in wet drips around my face.

Darkroom things. I knew all this stuff from when Dad had his own darkroom. How had I forgotten about it?

"The enlarger," I said, touching the big metal piece with a finger. I left a smeary print. "Trays. Tongs." There were no developers or fixers. Mom must have dumped those so she wouldn't have to store them.

"Where's your camera, Dad?" For a moment I expected him to answer. I sat back on my heels and closed my eyes. I waited, holding my breath, hoping. After a while I let out a long sigh, then pulled down the third box, bigger than the rest. More books, more darkroom equipment. And something heavy wrapped in an old blue blanket.

Here it was.

With care I released what I was looking for from the folds of the cloth. There were two cameras bodies wrapped up, snug against each other.

Dad's monster 6x7. I had forgotten about that. Now I was flooded with memories.

"Let me try," I had begged, pulling on Dad's arm at the elbow. "Let me try to take a picture."

"It's too heavy, Carolina."

We were at the beach, and it was wintertime. I must have been only seven or eight years old.

"I won't drop it." It was cold out. My nose felt almost frozen. The wind blew off the ocean hard, making me grimace. The water was gray-looking and capped with white foam.

"Just stand still a minute," Dad said. "I want to try for some shadow photographs." For some reason Mom and Madelaine weren't with us.

He snapped pictures of our two shadows, long and thin, footprints walking through them. And then shots of me alone, my arms raised in the air, making a circle like a ballerina. One of me pointing to the ocean with a stretched-out finger, standing on one foot. And then another of us together, me on his shoulders, my shadow arms making an X in the sand. He never let me shoot a picture.

I picked the camera up now. It was heavy and the wooden handle seemed almost warm in the heat of the attic. I held it, wishing for more memories of Dad and me shooting pictures together. There were none. How could there be more of something that rarely happened?

Then I unwrapped his old 35.

"This is what I want," I said. "This is it."

An old Canon, black and silver. All automatic. I sniffed the camera, hoping for the smell of Dad, but the only fragrances I could catch were that of my own sweat and metal.

I closed my eyes. I could almost hear Dad's voice. "Don't wiggle so much, Carolina. Madelaine, come on. You're twelve years old. Put your tongue back in your mouth. There. That's the look. Don't move."

I hugged the camera close to my chest. "Daddy," I whispered.

We really did have a good time when Dad was taking pictures. And the vacations—all for the sake of photography. Going to Ocala and St. Augustine and boating on the ocean. It was so much fun.

I couldn't help smiling.

I pulled out all the lenses that went with the camera, and all the filters, too. I felt a tiny burst of excitement at the thought of using Dad's camera equipment. He never would let me before.

Finally, I packed up the boxes one by one, putting them back the way Mom had had them. Then I started downstairs to clean up my new tools and to shower after my "sauna."

After I found the boxes, I started on a little dream. In it I could shoot pictures as well as Dad could. And he was real proud of me too.

"How many of you have cameras?" Ms. Field asked us. Ms. Field looked like a model, long sun-bleached hair, petite body, beautiful face.

"She's standing on the wrong side of the camera," I whispered to Garret.

He nodded. Then smiled at me. "So are you," he whispered back.

I felt my face flame, but it was an okay kind of flaming.

"You have to have a camera of your own, preferably a thirty-five-millimeter, the brand doesn't matter. Bring it to class tomorrow and don't forget it even once this term. As time goes on and you start shooting photographs, you'll be choosing your favorites to enlarge. Keep this in mind as you learn and take pictures."

"Hardnose," Mara said, leaning into Garret. She had chosen a seat on the other side of him. She grinned. "I'll have Dad go get me a camera today," she said.

"In the back," Ms. Field said. "Listen up. I don't want to have to repeat myself."

Mara nodded and I looked down at my desk.

"This is a camera," Ms. Field said, holding a Nikon on the palm of her hand.

"She's a bright one," Mara whispered.

I didn't answer. I didn't want to.

"And models like this, thirty-five millimeters, all work in the same way."

We went through the camera, piece by piece, and by the end of class, Ms. Field was handing out a worksheet to fill in on the parts of the camera.

Walking out of class, clutching her used paperback copy of *The Joy of Photography,* Mara said, "Oh, Garret. I'm never going to remember this all." She squeezed in between Garret and me, somehow pushing me away from my place. "You'll have to help me. I can't get behind on my very first day."

"Can't you study the pages she gave us?" I said. My blood seemed to have turned rancid or something where Mara was concerned. Hadn't I seen her do this very thing to lots of guys and their girlfriends? Hadn't I seen her work before? Wasn't she my friend? Would that matter at all?

"There's so much more than that. There's so much more," Mara said. She had Garret's arm now.

He looked at me over the top of her head.

I tried to smile, but my lips wouldn't work. They were frozen, it felt, so that they made a straight line.

"Carolina," Garret said.

What? I wanted to say, but all I could do was look at him. I felt my eyes tear up. Why couldn't I control my stupid feelings?

"How about you come over and we study, Garret?" Mara said. She glanced back at me. "You could come too, if you wanted. But we do have those two other classes together."

Still I didn't move. For some reason the pain of seeing Mara with Garret wrapped itself around my hidden pain of Madelaine. I wasn't even sure why.

"Madelaine," I whispered. If only she were here . . . I closed my eyes and turned away. It was time to go home. Mom had said she would wait in the back parking lot. She'd said we'd go get a snack or something.

"Carolina," Garret called.

I moved against a tide of people that was almost too strong to get through. I'd go out and find Mom. Then we'd go home together.

"Carolina." Garret's voice was in my ear, his hand warm on my arm. "You're going the wrong way."

I jerked to free myself, but Garret held on. "Let me go," I managed. I blinked my eyes. Things were swimming before me, people, lockers, the clock above the door at the end of the hall.

"Garret, Carolina," Mara said, her voice almost lost in the crowd trying to get away from school.

The door at the back of the hall opened and bright light cut into the fake light inside. I could smell sweat and perfume and I tasted my tears.

Garret stopped me. "It's okay, Carolina."

"Not to me, it isn't," I said.

"We're going to miss the bus." Mara's voice was sharp.

"Yeah," I said, pulling away. "The bus. And I'm riding home with Mom. So I've got to go." *Invite him,* my heart told my head, but I kept moving to get free.

"All right," he said.

"I've got to go."

Garret nodded. I remembered Ms. Field saying, "Start looking at what you want to photograph right now. Let your eye be the camera. See what looks good to you."

Garret looks good to me, I had thought. But Mara had said it. Out loud. To him.

"The bus," Mara screeched. The halls were thinning of people.

"I better go," I said, but I was thinking, *Tell him to come.*

"See you later then," Garret said, but he didn't move.

"We'll have to run," Mara said.

Tell him to come with you, I thought, *Mom won't mind.*

"Maybe we can do this together. Tonight. On the porch swing," he said. He was trying to look in my eyes, but I wouldn't let him.

"Maybe." I couldn't do it. I couldn't make myself see what was going to happen.

Mara was beside Garret then, tugging on his arm. "She can go home with her mother. *We* need to catch the bus." And she pulled him away.

"Yeah, bye," I said. *Oh, Madelaine. Daddy.* I squeezed my eyes shut a moment.

I started out again. "Daddy, I miss you." A pain came up in my chest, burning hot.

The door at the end of the hall opened again, the

light bright. Somebody came through. I blinked, leaning my head forward. She looked so much like . . .

"Madelaine," I whispered again. Then I shouted it out. "Madelaine."

I started to walk through the last few strays in the hall. Everything seemed so intense. I could hear the buzz of the fluorescent lights. Somebody slammed a locker door and I almost felt the echo.

"Carolina." Her voice . . .

"Dear God," I said. "It *is* you." My heart pounded, hard. I ran then, spilling my books to the floor and not caring. "Madelaine." My voice was almost a shriek.

Madelaine ran toward me, her hair bouncing back behind her shoulders. She was running too.

Tears streamed from my eyes.

And then Mom grabbed me tight by the shoulders.

"What?" I said. My eyes weren't seeing things right. "What?"

"It's me," Mom said.

"Mom," I said. "I thought you were . . ." Frustration made a bad taste come into my mouth. The air in the hall smelled stale. How could I tell her I thought something from a movie was happening to me? "You two look, I mean looked, so much the same."

"That's a compliment," Mom said. Her voice was

smooth, but I could tell her heart hurt. She tried to pull me into a hug, but I wouldn't let her.

There was a wall of tears waiting behind my disappointment. "I better get my books," I said.

In slow motion I walked back to where I had dropped things. Paper was scattered, my algebra homework crumpled. My notebook was bent backward and all the things I had put in it the night before were caught underneath. My photography book had fallen open to a page of a young mother with her two daughters at a fountain. I slammed the book shut so Mom wouldn't see.

But she had already.

"It takes time," she said.

I looked up at her from my crouch, then took in a deep breath.

"It takes time," she said again, and I wasn't sure if she was telling me that, or convincing herself.

I wonder at my mother. How does she have the strength?

I wonder at Mara. How does she have the nerve?

I wonder at myself. How am I going to make it?

Chapter 11

About seven-thirty that evening Garret came over. He had *The Joy of Photography* in his hands. He held the book up so I could see it through the screen door and said, "You want to study?"

Only you, I thought. *I want to study only you.* But I nodded, then started grinning like a fool.

Garret grinned back.

We stationed ourselves on the front porch swing with a can of Off! and a package of Nutter Butter Peanut Butter Sandwich Cookies and glasses of milk.

"Mom remembered these are my favorite snack," I said, crossing my legs under me and facing Garret.

"Yeah?" Garret's face looked a little funny.

I needed to explain. "Since the accident," I said.

"You know since Dad and Madelaine . . ." It was still hard to talk about.

"What about it?" he asked.

"She's just never, you know, remembered things like this. But she's changing." I opened the package of cookies. "It's good."

"Are you changing too?" Garret asked.

"Are you asking this for psychology class? Do you need material or a case study or something?" I teased him.

"Yesh, Mish McKinneyh. I am shtudying people who've . . ." Garret stopped talking, then took a cookie. He looked away.

"Go ahead," I said. "It was funny. Your doctor imitation was funny."

"I don't think so," Garret said. He took my hand in his, the one that held two uneaten cookies. "I think the whole thing just sucks."

My mouth waggled and I blinked fast. My voice came out a whisper. "It's been almost a year."

"I don't care how long it's been," Garret said. He'd closed his eyes like he was frustrated. "I compare myself to you and, Carolina, I couldn't do it."

"Oh yes you could," I said. "It's not like I had a choice."

"That's part of what makes it so crummy."

I looked hard at him, trying to see what he might really be thinking. Then I started whispering, "The thing is this: I keep telling myself it'll get easier. I keep telling myself not to expect them back. Garret, I keep hoping I might get to see them again, at least see Madelaine. You know, tell her goodbye. Tell her how much I miss her. And my dad."

Garret reached out his hand and smoothed my cheek. I rested my face on his palm.

"Oh, Carolina," he said. He kissed me then, soft tender kisses.

I heard Mom clear her throat and I moved away from Garret. She was in the living room.

"Mom?"

There was no answer; then she pushed open the door.

"Yes, Carolina." I looked at her. She smiled big. "Are you *studying*?" she asked.

"Nearly," I said.

Garret bowed his head. "Caught," he said.

I opened my photography book. "You sneak," I said loud enough for her to hear. I made it sound like I was kidding, but I wasn't. I felt afraid. Had she heard me? Had she heard about that bit of my heart?

Mom went back inside, still smiling.

"Your mom is cool," Garret said.

"Yeah, right," I said. "I'll ask you questions first. On your drawing there, show me the hot-shoe outlet."

Garret grinned, a wide show-all-your-teeth grin.

He kissed me again and, pointing to the book, said, "Okay, the hot-shoe outlet is right there."

"Wrong."

"Oh, darn." He didn't sound a bit disappointed.

We studied, exchanging kisses. By the end I felt I knew the camera body parts like I knew Garret's lips. Would I ever see another picture of an Olympus camera and not think of Garret?

The sun sank low and painted the clouds bright orange.

"That would make a great picture," I said.

Swallows dipped and dived in the front yard, snatching up mosquitoes for a late-night dinner. It wouldn't be too much longer before the bats were out.

I closed my book, then snuggled back onto Garret, resting full against him. His body was warm under mine. I watched the night birds dash around, swooping.

"I think high school's going to be all right," I said.

Garret wrapped his arms around me. His chin was on my head. "I told you you'd like it."

I closed my eyes, glad I hadn't bothered to turn on the light. Garret and I were disappearing from Mom's view as the day's light slipped away. I felt safe here on my porch. Safe in his arms. Photography class was far from me now and so was Mara. Sort of.

I loosed myself from Garret's hold. I turned and looked at him. I could only see his outline really.

"She used to be my friend," I said.

"Who, your mom?" At first I was startled by the question. Was Mom my friend again, like she had been? I pushed the thought away.

"Actually I was thinking about Mara."

"She still is."

"No," I said. "She's your friend. She wants to be more." In the dark I could say anything.

"She's okay."

"She's pretty and you know it."

"Pretty isn't everything."

A pain came up inside, that same pain that came up in unexpected places like in the shower, or during beautiful sunrises or at school watching my used-to-be best girlfriend.

"I don't get her," I said. "I kind of think she's going to do what I've watched her do to so many people. I keep hoping it won't happen. But it's like I'm watching her move into position."

"What are you talking about?"

"She wants you bad. And she doesn't care that I'm here." I waved my hands around in the air. At my feet my photography book pages rustled in a breeze that made a weak effort to push away mosquitoes. The fireflies flashed in the yard.

Garret was silent. Then he took both my hands and held them, soft, in his own. But he didn't say anything.

A Note to You

I opened up then, told Garret my deepest heart feelings. I told him about how I felt gypped that half my family was gone. I told him about how Dad didn't have to take Madelaine with him. I told him everything because I couldn't carry it along alone anymore. You wouldn't have said anything but, you see, I had to.

I talked and it seemed that getting all these words out soothed me.

And when Mrs. Harrison called him in to take a phone call, I was feeling okay.

Chapter 12

I decided to talk to Mara straight out. The next after-noon, after school, I rode my bike over to her house, shaking all the way. I felt so young, so much like a child.

Mara lives with her father in a mansion in the neighborhood where my whole family used to live.

As I pedaled into the yard, following the curvy driveway to the front porch, I wondered what it would be like to have your mom missing even if she lived in the same town the way Mara's did. How would I feel if Mom took off to live with another guy and start another family? How would I feel if they were in town here and she never had time for me? That was what was going on with Mara, but she never seemed to care.

I knocked on the door and waited for my friend. My used-to-be best friend.

Things will be all right, I thought. *You're going to work things out with her just fine.*

"Carolina!" Mara said when she saw it was me. She threw the door wide open. A blast of cold air hit me in the face.

"Hey," I said, but I didn't step in. I was so nervous I thought I might puke all over the tile entryway of her house. My mouth flapped a couple of times. "Mara, we need to talk."

She nodded and gave me a small smile. She seemed so sure of herself. Almost like a grown-up. "Come on in."

I swallowed a couple of times, then forced myself inside. This place that had been a haven for me was too cold, too lonely. We made our way through the long halls to Mara's room. Her house was as familiar as my own and I felt almost a loss at what might happen once we got to the Bra Sanctuary.

"Want something to eat?" she asked as I followed her. "Or do you want to go swimming?"

I shook my head. "No." My voice sounded weak. There were too many memories, laugh-your-guts-out memories here. It was hard to be normal. I had to get this out. "Just want to talk right now."

Mara plopped on the rose-colored carpet in her room and motioned for me to sit with her. Sunlight poured in through the glass door that led to the pool.

"What's up? Is high school killing you?"

I shook my head. "Not really. I think I'm gonna make it."

"I absolutely love it," Mara said. And she leaned her head back so her blond hair fell in a small pile on the floor. "I love the work, I love the choices. I love the guys. Lots of guys there. Not that *you* would notice, Carolina."

My cheeks felt cool. Was there something wrong with me? Had I been *imagining* Mara at work on Garret or was it true?

"I, um."

Mara stared at me, her eyes almost penetrating.

I picked at my thumbnail. "Every guy in the world likes you, Mara," I said.

"Yeah, right," she said. She laughed. I could tell she believed my words.

"But listen, okay?" My voice was breathy, my heart pounding. Could she tell? Did she know I was so nervous? "I really care about Garret."

Mara stopped her smiling. Her eyes narrowed a bit. "Is somebody after him, Carolina?"

Yeah, you are, I thought. *Stop making this so awkward.* But all I said was, "Well, I'm, uh . . ."

"Remember when I gave you all those bras?"

I nodded, grateful for a change in the conversation. Maybe I could think of something to say now.

"Remember how you only wanted to wear Madelaine's undershirts?" Mara didn't look at me now. "I'll let you in on a little secret. I thought that was kind of weird. Your dead sister's undershirts. I'm glad you're not into that anymore."

Wearing Madelaine's clothes had made me feel better. Not so alone. They'd been a comforter almost, wrapping me up in her smell and in her leftover memories. "They're too small for me now," I said. I was amazed I could talk with my breath all gone. My heart pounded hard. I could even feel the thumps in my face. What was this Madelaine thing going on here? We didn't talk about Madelaine and Dad—that had always been the unspoken deal.

Mara stood and went to her window. She peered out to the just-mowed backyard. "I'm glad you're growing out of the . . . accident."

My throat wasn't swallowing right. Something blocked it, but I'm not sure what.

"For a while there I thought maybe you would always hold on to it. That undershirt thing really freaked me out."

I nodded.

"So have you forgiven your father yet? For taking Madelaine on that little trip?" She turned and looked me in the eye, her head lowered a bit.

Without meaning to, I gasped. "I better go," I said. Her words felt like a knife, cutting into my heart. Somehow I made myself get to my feet. My legs had turned wooden. "I came here to talk about Garret, not my family."

Mara's eyes flashed. "Look, I'm not interested in your boyfriend, if that's what you think. If that's even what you call him. There are plenty of guys better than him."

"Not for me," I said, turning. I was so close to tears that my face felt full of water. "For you, Mara. You're perfect. You know what to say, and what to do with guys. But I don't. And I don't like the way you are with him."

"And what if he does?" Mara's question was so hot in my face it was like I had felt her breath.

"I'd like him to decide without your influence. You already know you can have him. Why don't you just leave me my one good thing?"

"You're starting to do what you used to do all the time, Carolina. You're crying."

She was right. I wiped at my face with both hands when what I wanted to do was fall to my knees and bawl. Everything Mara had said was like a sword in the gut. Now I wished I had puked on the floor.

"Quit acting like a baby. I'm pretty sure Garret's not old enough to handle you boobing all the time."

I was to the door now. I had to wipe my hands free of tears and sweat to get the knob to turn. "Just leave him alone, Mara," I said one last time.

Mara cursed at me, then slammed the door.

I got on my bike and started for home, pedaling slow, letting the hot winds of September dry my face till it felt like I'd put egg whites on my skin.

A Note to You

Anybody else would have known how to handle Mara, but I didn't. All I could do to relieve my guts, which seemed to be tied in knots, was pedal around town. And so I did, until it was almost dark. I missed dinner, I missed doing my homework. I missed Mom leaving to go teach her night class. I knew it would scare Mom, but I didn't care. I just rode my bike till I found myself on the beach where we all used to go before. I climbed off my bike and let it fall in the sand. Then I sat out there in the dark for a while, listening to the crash of the waves and almost hearing the voices of my family as we played there.

I kept remembering.

Mom doesn't know. She doesn't know I heard her and Dad that night and I know what she said before the trip to California.

Chapter

We were in the old house, all of us. The day had started out fine. We'd stayed that afternoon at the beach. Dad tried to teach me to body surf but the waves weren't strong enough. Mom and Madelaine argued about a dress Madelaine wanted for a dance that was coming up at school. The sun was hot, a slight breeze blew and everything was okay until we got into the car to come home.

"Let's stop and get something to eat," Mom told Dad.

There was sand on my feet and I was seeing how many white-sand footprints I could make on the blue carpeting on the floor.

"Not tonight," Dad said. "We ate out three times this week already."

Mom shifted in her seat. "I'm too tired to cook, Steven."

"And I'm tired of restaurants."

"Okay, you two," Madelaine said. Both of us could see where this was going. "No fighting."

"Stay out of this, Madelaine," Dad said. "It's none of your business. This is between your mom and me."

I cowered in the corner, waiting for the fight that would come for sure now.

"Why do you talk to her like that?" Mom asked. She was gritting her teeth. "Why are you so hateful?"

"This is an argument about eating out," Dad said. I could see his knuckles were white on the steering wheel.

"It was a good day," Madelaine said, pushing at Dad and Mom with her words. "But Carolina and I can always expect this grown-up bunch of crap from the two of you." Only she didn't say *crap*.

"What in the hell are you thinking about, talking that way?" Dad hollered.

And the fight was on.

Madelaine and I sat without speaking at dinner, listening to the two of them sending out barbs across the table at each other, like the tail of a stingray slaps back and forth. All at once Dad pushed his chair back. It fell to the floor. My stomach hurt and the Kentucky Fried Chicken Mom had "convinced" Dad to stop for tasted like greasy wood.

"I am so sick of this crap, Amelia," Dad shouted. His face was red and the veins in his neck stuck out. His voice seemed to shake the glasses we'd poured Coke into. "I've filed papers already, get it? I don't want to be married anymore. There are other things I want to do with my life, and you can rest assured they don't include spending a moment more here."

Now I couldn't chew.

Dad waved his arms around in the air like he was trying to keep his balance.

There were a few moments of silence and I heard the clock on the mantel in the living room wind up to dong the hour.

Mom set her fork down. She folded her hands under her chin and put an almost smile on her lips. "If you notice, Steven, I'm not stopping you from packing."

My swallower quit working.

"Jeez, Mom," Madelaine said. "Extra doses of compassion from both of you, huh?"

Mom didn't even look at my sister, but Dad did. Then he stormed out of the room, cursing as he went.

"Another fun evening at the McKinney residence," Madelaine said. "With food to match." She picked up a forkful of mashed potatoes and held them upside down. Nothing happened.

I giggled and looked at Madelaine. I could see her bottom lip shaking.

Mom kept up that crazy bit of a smile, not saying anything to either of us. I could hear Dad stomping around upstairs. My heart was pounding and I thought, *Divorce will be a relief after all this.*

"Carolina," Madelaine said. She was using a syrupy voice. One she knew bugged Mom a lot. "I love high school. Ninth grade is so much fun."

Dad's chair was on the floor still.

"School?" I said, taking Madelaine's cue. *We* didn't have to fight. "How can you like school? Eighth grade sucks big-time."

"How many times have I asked you two not to say 'suck'?" It was Mom. Her smile was gone. Her hands were clenched into fists.

"How many times have we asked you two not to fight like a couple of dogs?" Now Madelaine wore Mom's bit of a smile.

"Uh-oh," I said.

Madelaine smirked at Mom.

"Madelaine," Mom said, and she leaned forward. "Feel free to leave with your father." And then she was gone from the table.

"Love at home," Madelaine said. And she started singing words from an old church song. She looked over at me. "Join in," she said.

I shook my head. "Isn't this chicken finger-lickin' good?" I asked, and we both laughed so hard I thought I was going to wet my pants.

That night, after everybody got in bed, the fight started again. My room was closest to Mom and Dad's and I could hear their voices, loud, coming down the hall at me. Did they think we were asleep? Did they even care?

Not again, I thought. I crept out of bed and went to the phone in the hall that Madelaine and I shared. I called Mara. She answered on the third ring. "They're at it again."

"I sure am sorry, Carolina," Mara said. Her mom had left home only a month before.

"He said he sent in papers already."

"Divorce papers," Mara said. She knew everything.

I nodded even though she couldn't see me.

"Are you sad?"

"No," I said. "I think I'm relieved."

We talked for a few minutes more, until the bedroom door down the hall was flung open. I heard it smack against the wall.

"Gotta go," I whispered, and hung up fast. I crept as fast as I could to my room and sat in the darkness of the doorway.

"I'll take who I want," Dad said. "Either girl. Both of them if they both want to."

"So you'll make them choose."

"I've put as many hours in those two as you have."

"Only lately," Mom said. "Not when they were little."

"Don't get in my way, Amelia," Dad said, and I could tell by his voice he was talking about the who-ever-got-to-go-with-him fight. "They're my children too. I love them as much as you do."

"They're not property," Mom said.

"And just what do you think I should do? Leave them here for you?"

Mom was silent a moment. "Leave Carolina," she said. "I'm not so sure I can handle Madelaine right now."

A cold feeling sank into my chest. I crawled out of my room on my hands and knees and headed toward Madelaine's room.

Her door was opened a crack. I butted at it with my head and moved to the side of her bed.

"Madelaine," I whispered.

She started awake with a "What?"

I laughed a little but what I really wanted to do was cry. "They're fighting about us now."

Madelaine stretched. Then she held back the covers with one arm. "Climb on in here with me," she said. "We can talk until you're sleepy or until they shut up."

"They want to separate us," I said.

Madelaine wrapped her arms around me and scrooched close to my back. "We'll never let them," she said, her voice soft in my hair. "I swear it on a stack of Holy Bibles."

A Note to You

Madelaine, why didn't you keep your promise to me?
Why did you go with Daddy? Why did you have to follow
him to the very end? You've left me here so alone that some-
times I feel like fragile glass blown too thin, just waiting to
crack.

"I hope not," I said. "I think we're the only two
sane people in the family. You know, this is what happened to Mara, only her mother didn't care about her.
But I mean all the fighting stuff."

"Can you blame her for not caring?" Madelaine said
in a sleepy voice. "I don't like Mara either."

I laughed, letting my older sister's words calm me.
Now the harshness of what my parents were going
through wasn't as awful to my sore heart. Madelaine
and I would stick together, no matter what. I knew
that as I lay there next to her, her three-day-old
shaved leg hairs poking at me.

I talked until Madelaine started to snore.

"Madelaine," I said, shaking her awake. "I'm
almost done talking. I sure am glad you're my
friend."

"I love you too, Carolina."

I grinned in the dark, wondering if my teeth glowed. Then, because the fight down the hall was over, I went to sleep in my sister's arms, safe.

The memory is a perfect one, except for the fight. Madelaine and me all snuggled in her bed. Outside the window a pale streak of moon shone and every once in a while I saw a lightning bug blink.

If there had been a way, I would have snapped that picture of the two of us close together. I would have used black-and-white film because those are the colors I remember and Ms. Field says black-and-white photography can be dramatic.

And I would have gotten a close-up, too, of my sister asleep.

But, of course, I didn't know I should. And Dad wouldn't have let me use his camera anyway.

Chapter 14

It only took a few days before I felt comfortable at New Smyrna High School. It took that same amount of time for classes to become mundane. The only two I looked forward to were English and photography, and that's because Garret was there.

In English I spent lots of time writing in my journal. Dr. Morris was right. Saying things, putting them down on paper, was soothing. No wonder I had become such a good letter writer to Garret while he was gone. No wonder I had letters to my family stashed in envelopes in my room.

But the class that caused me joy and anxiety was photography.

"Groups of three," Ms. Field would sometimes say,

and Mara would grab a tight hold on Garret, who already had my hand. Then we would study together, or quiz each other on depth of field or lighting shots.

"Twos," Ms. Field would call out. Mara would latch on to Garret faster than I could even blink my eye. But there was no way I was going to leap for him. I wanted it to seem like I had more dignity than that, even if I didn't.

On the bus, Mara was there, squeezing in next to Garret and me, trying for my place.

"Don't you notice it?" I asked him one afternoon when we'd gotten off the bus and left Mara staring out the window at us.

"I see she doesn't like you anymore," he said.

"And you know she likes you?"

He nodded a little. "But I'd rather not think about it."

"How do you know?" We were walking home together, holding hands. Garret's hand seemed dry after a day in school, like he hadn't wiped off chalk dust from math class or something.

"Oh, she's told me."

I jerked Garret to a halt. The sun was shining down hard. I could smell the tar in the street. "What did she say?"

Garret gave me the old eyeball. "You know. The usual."

"I don't know," I said. And I prayed it wasn't any

of the lines Mara used to say she said to guys when we were friends.

"What a stud I am. How strong I look. How I should be a model."

My mouth dropped open. "Really?"

"No, Carolina," Garret said, and he laughed. "She's just told me she likes me. She's told me she wishes you and I weren't such good friends."

"And?" I said.

"And she's available when we're, you know, done. Or whatever."

"Done?" I said. I felt like I had lost all ability to say more than one word at a time.

"Are we going to be done soon?" I asked. Now the sun seemed too bright and I had to shade my eyes.

"I don't know," Garret said. "Are we?"

"Do you want to be?"

"No. Do you, Carolina? She said . . . Do you?" Garret had leaned forward toward me and I could smell his gum. In the dried-out grasses in the ditch next to us, grasshoppers clicked out little tunes.

"What did she say?"

"Nothing really."

I started us walking again. I needed to get out of the sun. My throat was dry and I was sweating. "Let's go get a drink." Lemonade would be good. Real lemonade. With lots of sugar and crushed ice. "You can tell me while we walk."

"Just that you go through guys fast. That you'd get tired of me."

"She said I do that?" I laughed, then shook my head. Garret and I walked past the hibiscus bushes that were covered in big red flowers, then up my driveway. "Is that all?"

"Yeah."

"And what did you say?"

We were to the door now.

"I told her I guessed I'd have to wait for that to happen. That I like you a lot and I'm not planning on going anywhere unless you tell me to."

"Oh, thank you, Garret," I said, and slung my arms around his neck.

We took pictures that afternoon of the flowers in Mom's overgrown beds, until the sun was too low for shots without a flash. Every once in a while I caught Mom looking at us through the curtains. Once she waved, smiling. I pretended I didn't see her and she disappeared for good from the window.

I felt bugged inside. Almost like Mom was coming into a place where she wasn't allowed. "I thought she'd forgotten how to do anything except work," I told Garret. "Now it feels like all she does is hover."

"Maybe that's how moms get," Garret said. "I think my mom has forgotten how to make breakfast. Whatever you do, don't be the last of five boys or your mom goes gray and starts babying you all the time. Except for breakfast."

"Well, whatever you do, don't be the only daughter left after a serious plane crash or your mother goes gray, then disappears for a year."

Garret quit snapping pictures and looked over at me.

"Sorry," I said. "It sounded funny in my mind."

Night fell and Garret and I went out onto the front porch swing. Overhead, Mom's baskets of petunias, newly planted, made darker splashes on a growing-dark sky. Garret's feet scuffed at the wooden porch floor. I could hear sand under his shoes.

I snuggled into his arms.

And then Mara appeared, out of the bushes it seemed.

"Garret," she said. "I need help. I need you." It sounded like she had been crying.

The hair on the back of my neck stood up even though a hot breeze blew. We'd be using the air conditioner tonight.

"What's the matter, Mara?" Garret asked. His hold tightened around me.

"It's that test in algebra. There's no way I'm going to pass. Will you help me study for it?"

Garret didn't move for a second. I felt his breath rush out in a sigh.

"Please, Garret," Mara said.

"You better go," I said at last.

"Oh, Carolina," Mara said. "I didn't know you were here."

"Why wouldn't I be, Mara?" I said. "This is my house."

"You don't have to be such a witch," Mara said. "I'm scared. And Garret's the only place I have to turn."

You sound like a soap opera, I thought, but I didn't say anything.

"It's getting late, Mara," Garret said, but he stood up anyway, pulling me with him. He turned and in the dark I could almost see him. He hugged me close. "I'll come get you in the morning." His voice was a whisper.

I watched Garret and Mara leave. Then I went inside to sit with Mom, who'd heard the whole thing but had nothing to say about it except, "I'm sorry."

Chapter

I am sitting at the desk in my room looking at myself in a mirror that hasn't always been there. I have the feeling that Garret was just over and I almost feel good about that.

My room is dark, all around dark, except for right where I sit. Here there is light, but it's soft light, like the moon sometimes is. Everything's in black and white, like an old-timey movie or a good photograph.

I stare at my reflection, and then there she is, Madelaine, standing behind me.

"I didn't hear you come in," I say.

"I snuck through the window," she says. And even though my room is on the second floor this doesn't seem weird to me.

Madelaine comes up near and leans down close. I smell Mom's White Shoulders.

"Mom might not like it that you have on her perfume," I say, and Madelaine smiles.

"Dad's waiting, so I can only stay a minute," she says.

A cold feeling comes into my stomach. It seeps out into my arms and legs.

"You're not leaving, are you?" I ask.

Madelaine smiles and I watch our reflection there together. "A minute," she says. "I'm staying a minute."

For some reason I start crying. "I think I need you around longer than a minute," I say. Tears run down my face, shiny like aluminum foil.

"It's all right," Madelaine says.

"No it isn't," I say. "I miss you so much."

The tears have made a puddle on my desk and my hands are stuck in the wetness. "If I could just hug you again. You and Daddy."

"That's not possible," Madelaine says, but she keeps on smiling.

The tears are so bright now, so bright.

"Madelaine." It's Daddy's voice. I haven't heard his voice in such a long time. That voice. Now I am crying harder. Crying bright, aluminum foil tears.

Madelaine leans closer.

"I miss you so much," I say.

"I miss you too, Care."

The pain caused by my nickname makes me put my head down on my desk. I haven't heard that in such a long time. I am heavy with grief.

"We've got to leave," Daddy says. "Kiss your sister fast, hug your mom. We can't miss this flight."

"Don't go this time, Madelaine," I say, only I'm having a hard time talking. It's like everything is in slow motion. "Don't go this time."

"It'll be fun, Carolina," Dad says from the dark of the room. I can't see anything of him except his outline. "We're going to have a blast."

A blast. "Don't go."

A *blast*. "Please don't go."

Madelaine reaches out her hand, reaches it out in slow motion toward my shoulder. If she will just touch me one more time maybe I'll be able to make it the rest of my life.

"You're going to be all right," she whispers.

"Please," I say. "I love you."

But the words get mixed up in my bright tears and I'm not sure Madelaine hears me, though she never stops smiling, not even when she turns away and leaves me there at my desk.

I woke up crying. I felt strangled from sadness. My hands were wet with sweat.

"Oooh," I said. "Oooh."

A Note to You

It had been so real, the dream. Have you had them like that? So real that when you wake up it's like things are still going on. And the tears you've been crying still wet your cheek, or the laughter you've been laughing still sounds in the air. It was like that, only when I woke up I had the memory of the telephone call trying to edge into my mind as well as everything else. The call telling us that things hadn't gone well with the flight. The call that took everything normal from my mother and me.

The streetlight cast a faint orange glow through my window. I could see that the light was on in the bathroom down the hall.

I squeezed my eyes shut and tried to settle back to sleep, but my body was cold from the dream and every part of me seemed to ache.

"Oh, Madelaine, Madelaine."

I lay motionless for a few minutes, then realized there was no way it would work. I couldn't sleep. At least not right now. So I thought of my sister, tried to bring her image up in my mind. She was hazy. I tried a memory, something I had felt over, like your tongue does a tooth when it's bothering you.

It came at last, Madelaine and me in the playroom of our old house, playing dress-up.

"You're Snow White," I remembered Madelaine saying. I closed my eyes to make things more clear, so I could get every bit from this memory. "And I'm Rose Red."

"You're always Rose Red." Me. We were little. Maybe six and eight.

"Wear this around your head," Madelaine said. "Like it's long hair." She pinned a towel under my chin. Downstairs I heard a door slam and then Dad's angry voice.

"They're fighting again," I said. The towel was a little tight.

Madelaine closed the playroom door hard. "We don't need 'em," she said. "And in this story the mom and dad are nice."

"Yeah," I had said. "Nice."

"Now, here's a broom. You get to dance with that when we go to the ball. It's your Prince Charming."

"I want the mop this time. It has better hair," I said. "You always get the mop."

"I'm oldest and it's my story." Madelaine began humming a song and we twirled around the room with our dance partners.

It's funny that I knew there wasn't really a Prince Charming, at least not in our house, even at that young age.

When the cold feeling left, I got out of bed and padded over to the window. There was no breeze tonight. Mom had turned on the air conditioner. Air blew cool up through the vent at my feet, whisper soft.

I peered outside, toward Garret's house. And there he stood in his front yard, looking into the darkness across the street.

Without thinking, I threw open my window. "Garret," I called. My voice seemed to carry out into the night air, past the privet hedge, past the berm of azaleas Mrs. Harrison had planted a million years ago, past a small fountain of a child carrying a squirting fish.

Garret turned, startled, in the night. "What?"

I laughed, a bit of sadness loosening up from around my heart. "I'm in my room," I said. "What are you doing out there? It's so late."

Garret started toward my house, toward me. He looked back over his shoulder once.

Do you still like me? I wanted to say. *I feel so hurt about everything, but I'm not sure what's happened, or how to stop it.*

Even my thoughts made no sense, and I was the one thinking them. A sudden piece of happiness pierced my heart as I watched Garret push sideways through the fence the hedge made.

"Carolina," he said when he stood under my window.

"What are you doing up so late?"

"I guess I didn't know what time it was."

I looked at the clock near my bed. The glowing numbers read 3:23. "It's almost morning," I said. "Have you been up since you left here tonight? I mean, last night?" Seeing Garret made the iciness from my dream melt away. I leaned on the windowsill and waited for him to answer.

"Yeah," he said, ducking his head a bit. "I have." Then he looked up to where I stood. I couldn't see his face at all because it was dark.

"School starts in a few hours." I kept my voice low and knelt on the wood of the floor. My toes cracked.

"It's gonna be a long day." His voice was low.

"You better go to bed."

Garret was quiet a moment.

Or let me come down there and stand with you, I thought. *Let me rest my head on your shoulder again, like I did this evening on the front porch. Let me review camera body parts with you . . . or other things.* My imaginings made me smile, made my cheeks turn pink in the night.

"Carolina," Garret said, and his voice was sweet sounding. "You know, I'm not what you think I am."

"Huh?" The icy feeling started to creep in again, the way ice edges a puddle of water in February. "What do you mean?"

"I'm just not what you're thinking I am."

The air conditioner kicked off then. My room seemed especially quiet. Outside was quiet too. It was like everything had died for a moment.

"Have you ever been?" I asked, my voice cracking.

He looked down at the ground, then back up again. "Yeah," he said. "Yeah."

Please help me, God, I thought, and then I said, "Will you ever be again? What I think . . . I mean, what I thought you were?"

Garret spun around, away. "How the hell should I know, Carolina? How the hell should I know?" And then he took off running toward the privet hedge. He busted through, fighting the tight growth of the bushes. For a little bit I couldn't see him at all, just heard him running; then he was in my sight again. He sprinted down his sidewalk, jumped up on the porch and slammed inside his house.

"Oh," I said.

I am so alone sometimes I wonder at it. This ache seems all-consuming. And I had thought, somehow, that Garret would make it better for me. Or that time would. Or even Mom and her promise that she would be there for me.

Lying in bed that early morning I came to a cold realization: I was going to have to heal myself.

Chapter 16

"What in the world?"

That was the first thing I thought in the morning. I opened my eyes, and there, lying in bed, I wondered at what had happened.

Why had Garret run off like that? It was like he was mad. What was he mad at? Me? Had I done something? Had I said something wrong?

After a while I forced myself up and went in to shower. My knee was better, all healed up and haired over, Dad would have said.

I looked at myself in the mirror. "It was fine when he left last night. What happened?"

And that dream. What about that dream? I got into the shower and hoped for the hot water to smooth away my cares but it didn't work. I felt tormented at every corner of my mind. There was no relief. I cried, sitting down in the tub, and let the hot water rush over me, thinking how close I had been to seeing Madelaine again.

"What's the matter with you?" Mom asked when I came downstairs.

I shrugged. "I had a weird dream."

"What about?" Mom puttered around the kitchen. Something she hasn't done forever. She looked funny too. Funny around the eyes. "Do you want cereal?"

I shook my head. "I usually have toast and juice."

"I can do that," Mom said, and it almost sounded like she'd have to make an effort.

I kind of didn't listen to Mom, wondering when Garret would be over to pick me up. The bus would be coming soon, in fifteen minutes. Why wasn't he here yet? He usually came over a few minutes early.

"How's school?" Mom asked, interrupting my thoughts and handing over toast, a little too pale for me. "It's been more than a month now."

"Okay," I said. I didn't want Mom in my life right this second. Where was Garret?

"How's photography?"

The smell of toast filled the kitchen and I could smell Mom's coffee too. The chair seemed too hard under my bottom. I crossed one leg beneath me.

"Good," I said. "I love it. I know why Dad took so many pictures."

Mom paused a moment, then said, "It's an expensive hobby."

"Yeah." But there was something about capturing someone or something on film. You had it forever after, when you did that. "I'm thinking maybe of staying with it." I finished up a piece of the dry toast. "I'm thinking about making it a part of a career."

"Is that so?" Mom's eyebrows were raised and I could see she was way interested in what I had said. But I didn't have time for that now.

Minute by minute I checked the clock on the microwave. I could hear the spoon in Mom's coffee cup, clinking as she stirred, and then the sound of her sipping.

"I better go," I said at last.

Mom glanced up. "Can I take you to school, Carolina?" she asked, and her eyes filled with tears.

"I'll be okay," I said. "I'd rather take the bus." I couldn't look at her. Why was she getting ready to bawl? Did she know about last night?

I pushed the chair out from the table and it made a terrible screeching sound. Without looking back, I rushed out of the house.

"Goodbye," I called from the screen door.

"Goodbye, Carolina," Mom said. There were tears

in her voice. "I love you, honey." I heard Mom push away from the table too. She was coming after me.

I ran to the hedge, stopping to glance back toward the house. Mom stood at the door, staring after me. I hurried out of her sight.

The air felt heavy and was warm.

"She's too needy," I said, and tried to shrug off the way Mom had looked and sounded.

I walked in slow motion past Garret's house, looking for any movement behind the curtains, waiting for him to run out after me. But he didn't.

I shifted my book bag and went on down the street, which was speckled with early-morning sunlight and long shadows. Down I went, past the sign that read Ellison Acres in fancy script. Past the private drive that hid the house that Garret said he and I would get.

"What happened?" I asked no one. "Why didn't he come for me?" At the back of my head I could feel answers sitting and waiting, but I didn't really want to know why Garret hadn't come to get me and why Mom acted so strange.

Up ahead was the bus stop. A few kids stood under an oak tree that dripped Spanish moss. Past them I could hear the bus coming, switching gears as it made its way through our residential area, coming closer to me. Still there was no Garret.

I got on the bus. What about Mara? Would she be getting on at her stop?

It seemed to take an eternity to go the mile to Mara's place. Before we even came to a halt, I could see she wasn't there. Only two other people waited.

And then it clicked into place.

They had left together, from my swing, last night.

My face felt suddenly cool.

They had studied together last night.

"Oh, great," I said. I dropped my head into my hands. "Oh, great."

Cynthia Stonehocker, who I'd sat next to, glanced up from an abridged version of *Great Expectations*. "What's the matter, Carolina? Forget your homework?"

I looked into her big blue eyes. "No," I said. "I think I forgot my mind."

We chatted the rest of the way to school because I was sure if I didn't have something to do I might start bawling right then and there.

They weren't at school, either one of them.

In English I tried to listen to Dr. Morris, but it was even harder now than when I had Garret to stare at and dream about.

What were they doing?

In photography I sat alone at the large square table that Garret and Mara and I had shared. I felt conspicuous, like maybe everybody in class knew that

I had seen my boyfriend and used-to-be best friend walk off together the night before.

I went through pictures I had taken with Garret and Mara a while before in the horse pasture. We had climbed the barbed-wire fence and stood in the knee-high grass and leftover summer flowers, dressed in country-looking clothes. It had been my fashion shoot, and I wanted an old-timey look.

Mara wore a white cotton dress and a straw hat her mom had left behind.

Garret's pinstriped shirt was unbuttoned at the collar and the sleeves had been rolled back.

There was a picture, one I was sure would be good right when I snapped it, that ate at me. In this shot Garret looked at the camera, with a shy, tipped-head stare. And Mara, hat in hand, the wind blowing her hair just a bit, gazed at him. It was her look that felt like a knife in my guts.

"Nice work, Carolina." Ms. Field stood behind me. "The framing is good and the look soft."

"I used a piece of tricot," I said. "Like you told us."

"Good choice using the black-and-white film. It's a hard medium but it worked."

"Thank you," I said.

"This picture's worth blowing up. Think about it as a choice," Ms. Field said, and moved on to the next table.

I want to blow it up. Or tear it into a million pieces, I

thought. But a ripped-up picture wouldn't change the facts: Garret and Mara left together last night and they were still gone.

I searched through the rest of the black-and-white images. Some were too soft. In some the staging wasn't quite right.

The last picture was one of Garret and me. I had practically begged Mara to take it.

"Come on, Mara," Garret had said at last. "It's only one picture."

"But it won't count in class for me." Mara pouted when she spoke, her full lips appearing even fuller.

"Sure it will," I said. "Since I'm in the picture, Ms. Field will know *I* didn't take it."

Mara had stomped to my camera and whined about the dials that Dad's equipment had. For sure it was an older piece.

"She'll cut my head off, wait and see," I had said to Garret, my voice soft.

"No she won't," Garret said. "I won't let her." He wrapped his arms around me from the back and snuggled me in close at the waist. He brought his face close to mine and for a moment I thought he might kiss me.

I laughed. There was no way she could mess this picture up without Garret knowing.

"One, two, three," Mara had called, and I heard the camera click.

Now I pulled the picture out and laid it alongside the one of Mara and Garret.

He appeared happy, his face pressed close to mine. His shoulders hunched down. It almost seemed as if we were connected, he had rolled himself in that tight. And I was happy, a laugh having just escaped my lips. It was like we were a bundle, like we were supposed to be together.

And while Garret and Mara looked great, there was a spark missing from his part of the picture that Mara's enthusiasm couldn't cover up. Studying these two photos side by side, it was clear that Garret cared about me.

At least he had a week and a half ago.

I looked up to the front of the room. Ms. Field had written on the board in large block letters, "Choose your blowup today—Oct. 16!!!"

◆ ◆ ◆

A Note to You

What had I done? What had I done? How could I do this? I'm a traitor. How could I? For a moment there were no words in my head, only a blankness. I couldn't move. October 16 pounded on my head like a huge hammer. And then there was that phone call going through my mind, the call from the airport again. And Mom screaming and screaming and falling to the floor in a pile.

I felt frozen.

My throat closed up tight.

No wonder Mom had been such a crybaby. *Oh, Mom. I'm so sorry.*

How had I gone through the day not realizing? Had last night's deal messed up my head so bad I couldn't even think straight?

"I've got to go." I said this to no one; then I stood up and, tripping over my chair, made my way to the front of the class.

Ms. Field, who stood waiting next to her desk, watched me come toward her and stepped out to meet me.

"I've gotta go," I said. "I've really . . ." I couldn't speak. It felt like my lips had gone numb.

Ms. Field nodded and reached to take my arm. "Do you need help?"

I shook my head. "I need my mom," I whispered.

"I'll call ahead, tell the office you're coming."

I walked out into the hall, almost staggering. Behind me, I heard the intercom in Ms. Field's class buzz in and the office lady say "Yes?"

Had I been trying to forget? How could I forget? What was wrong with me?

In the office the air seemed too cold. But Mom had said she'd come get me when I called her out of class.

My head started pounding and by the time my

mother pulled up outside the school I had a terrible headache. But I deserved more than that, because today it was a year. A year since Mom and I found out there were no survivors on flight 293.

I decided later that afternoon I must have just been trying to block the worst day of my life out of my head. Why else would I have forgotten? It's not like I didn't know. Especially with all those hints from Mom.

I beat myself up about that for a long time. Then I went to bed, and to torture myself, I looked at the press releases from the accident.

When it got really late I stood at my window, staring past Garret's house. "I'll never forget again, Madelaine," I said. The window steamed up and I drew an X through the circle of moisture.

And then, right before I fell asleep, I got the extraordinary feeling that Madelaine was close by. That all I had to do was reach out and touch her and she'd be there. I lay quiet, not moving at all, so I could keep that feeling with me as long as possible.

Chapter

Garret didn't come by for me the next day for school, even though he was in English. And I didn't have the nerve to go looking for him.

A Note to You

What a baby. I can hear you saying that. "Carolina, go talk to him, you scaredy-cat. Find out what's going on." But I was a scaredy-cat before and I still am. Afraid to take dares, even ones from my mind.

"Look at your sister," Dad would say. "She's not afraid to try in-line skating." Or "Madelaine's doing a back flip now. You try, too, Carolina." All three of us would be up

there jumping on the trampoline and Mom would be on the ground saying, "You don't have to do anything you don't want, baby."

At least there's this about me: I've never been afraid to tell anyone that I am a scaredy-cat.

That's the main reason I didn't go on the plane. So there you have it.

I sat beside Garret and cast glances at him. At the end of class he turned to me. *Oh no.* I wanted him to talk to me and I didn't want him to talk to me.

"Carolina."

My mouth opened up and words poured out while I gathered my books. I couldn't seem to control them. "I missed you yesterday. And this morning, too. I waited for you at home, but I guess you stayed up way too late the other night, huh? I hope you're not sick or anything. Or Mara. Isn't it funny that you both missed on the same day? Well, I gotta go. I shouldn't be late for my next class. Mrs. Maxwell hates it when we're late."

I hurried out of class.

"Wait for me," Garret said.

"You better run along," I said over my shoulder. I sounded like my great-grandmother. I pushed through the hall crowds.

"I'll see you in photography," I heard Garret call out, but I didn't answer him.

Photography with Garret, my used-to-be boy-friend, and Mara, my used-to-be girlfriend. I didn't know if I could stomach it.

I wanted to leave early, but that wouldn't work. I'd already walked out of class the day before. So instead, I went through the motions of school. I answered all the questions I was supposed to, even volunteering information before being called on. And I dreaded every moment of the few hours between English and photography.

As I walked down the hall to our final class, my heart began to pound. A fine sweat broke out on my forehead and my hands started shaking.

Would anyone notice if I chose to sit somewhere else? Of course. With all the noise Mara made, with all the comments Ms. Field always threw in our direction, it would be obvious to people that I had made a change.

I came through the door. I could see both Mara and Garret from where I stood. He sat looking at his folded hands and she leaned close to him, saying something in his ear. When she saw me, Mara touched Garret with her fingertips. He gazed at her, not knowing I was in the room.

You can do this. You've done worse.

Ms. Field came up to me.

"Feeling better, Carolina?" she asked.

"Sort of," I said. I could smell the soft hint of her perfume.

"I put all your things on my desk."

"Thanks," I said, and looked my teacher in the eye. "I appreciate it. Sorry about yesterday. Things kind of got to me." Memories. Awful memories.

Ms. Field nodded. "Go ahead and sit down, we'll start."

Let me stay up here with you, I thought. In slow motion I started down the aisle, toward my place.

"All right, class," Ms. Field said. "Pop quiz."

People groaned. Jeff Hill booed as I walked past him, and Fern Caka mumbled, "This class was supposed to be easy."

At my table I could see Mara leaning over toward Garret, her mouth shaped like a small O. But now he watched me.

"Pop quizzes are part of the program," Ms. Field said, handing out the test. "If you want to be a good photographer, you need to know what you're doing. Knowledge is the key to power."

"But this is only a half-credit class," Fern said.

"Don't whine, Ms. Caka," Ms. Field said.

I sat down, trying to stay as far away from Garret as I could. He turned to face me and Mara put her hands on his shoulders, then peeked over him.

"Hi," she said. There was a look in her eye I

couldn't quite describe, one that seemed almost triumphant.

You're imagining things, I told myself. "Hey," I said, and got busy pretending to find a pencil. "Missed you guys yesterday." What was I doing?

Garret nodded, but Mara was ready. "We studied so long the night before, neither one of us could get up."

My stomach clenched.

"We weren't together when you saw me," Garret said, and his voice was low.

Mara moved close to Garret's face. "I just needed help," she told me.

"Seats, please," Ms. Field said. "Hands to yourself." Pale pink paper swished over the table. I took a quiz and started working.

"I hope I know these answers," Mara said.

"No talking," Ms. Field said.

"Maybe that study time will pay off," Mara whispered now, and stared right at me.

Garret didn't say anything, only looked at the test paper. The tops of his ears turned red.

"Yeah," I said. "Maybe."

The test was an easy one, a review of the things we had been learning over the past month of school. Questions on lighting and depth of field, as well as camera parts, filled the paper. I answered almost without thinking. But my mind buzzed with questions of my own.

Had Garret been with Mara so late the night before last? Was it her he was looking after at three-something in the morning?

I felt embarrassed for being so stupid. Of course it was. That's why he'd been mad at *me,* though why he would be made no sense at all.

After the quiz was over, Ms. Field taught about centering or not centering images. We looked at some Ansel Adams stuff and talked a little about black-and-white photography and I worried. There was still the bus ride home.

And that was just awful.

Mara clung to Garret all the way out the doors of the school. She almost didn't make it on the bus 'cause there wasn't enough room for them side by side.

"Stay with me," Garret said, and his voice was almost desperate, but I sat right behind Mrs. Huff and ignored him.

"She doesn't like us anymore," Mara said, and the two of them went to sit in the back.

And she was right about that. Well, half right.

It's funny how you can put things aside when you need to. I mean, I've been doing that for more than a year now. You know, about Madelaine and Dad. So I knew I could do it with this simple problem.

The only thing was that all this pain was like a multiplication problem going on in my head, getting bigger and bigger. All the huge pains from before were getting mashed in with this new emotion. I felt like a bottle being filled too full, uncomfortable and sad and ready to bust wide open, though I knew I'd never let that happen.

Chapter 18

"What are the chances," I asked Mom when we went out to dinner that night, "that I could change schools?"

"Huh?" Mom's eyes were red. She played with her hot-and-sour soup, stirring it around and around with a fat Chinese spoon. I guess she still wasn't over yesterday. I felt a pang of guilt, but I pushed it aside.

"I'm thinking maybe the Catholic school, you know that private place we pass on the way to McDonald's." My egg rolls were crisp and a little greasy. I poured a small pool of soy sauce onto my plate and it spread out thin and dark. I could smell ginger.

"You're not Catholic."

I nodded and bit into the egg roll. It was hot and steam escaped in a curl. "I don't think that will matter."

"It matters to me," Mom said.

"Religion never has before," I said. I sipped at fragrant tea that I had sweetened with packaged sugar.

"You're right," Mom said after a moment. "But for some reason I think it should at this moment."

"Because I want to go to a *Catholic* school?"

"No, because you want to go to a *private* school. An *expensive* private school."

"Oh."

"I don't know that I can afford to send you there." Mom leaned toward me. "What's going on, Carolina?" She reached for my hand, but I wouldn't let her take it.

"I think I need a . . ." I waved the egg roll around. "A change or something. You know, like fresh air."

The waitress, a tall redheaded woman squished into a blue-green shiny dress, brought a bowl of ham fried rice and a steaming plate of moo goo gai pan to the table.

"Thanks," Mom said, and she pulled her hand away from me. "What do you need fresh air for? You've only been in school for a month and a half."

"Yeah," I said. "So?"

"Carolina," Mom said. And her voice got all soft. She paused a moment. Her eyes teared up and she grabbed at a napkin. "Sorry."

I clenched my teeth. At this point in my life I really wouldn't be able to stand it if she cried. I felt like giving her advice. *Stand in the shower to cry, Mom, like I do.* Or *Look, I know it hurts, but wait till late at night to bawl. I can't handle it right now.*

And I couldn't, either. I was tired of missing Dad. Tired of missing Madelaine. And pained all through my guts for missing the little bit of time I had had with Garret.

Mom sucked in a big breath of air through her nose. "Is it Garret?"

I felt my face flash cool. How did she know? I wanted to say, *Yes, yes, oh, Mommy, yes.* But my mouth would only come up with one word: "Garret?"

My mother started eating then. The smile on her lips seemed to tremble as she ate. "And Mara?"

"Well," I said, giving in a little, "you know Mara."

"I thought I did."

"Madelaine never liked her. She used to always say she could see right through Mara."

"Really? I'm not surprised at that. Madelaine had a lot of insight about people. She always knew about your father and me . . ." Mom stopped short.

I gave her a look. "Everyone knew about you and Dad, Mom. You fought all the time."

Mom tipped her head. She reminded me of a bird, the way she sat on the edge of her chair, her whole body seeming to tremble, cocking her head like that.

"It's funny what death does," she said after a moment. "I know things weren't perfect between us, but I kind of remember them that way."

"Are you kidding?" I said. There was this place in me, kind of near Garret and Mara, that felt mean. "You don't remember all those fights? The screaming and hollering. And it was you who told Dad to take Madelaine . . ." Now *I* stopped. I hadn't meant to go that far. But I was so mad. It dawned on me as we sat at the table in that dinky restaurant, that it was Mom's fault Madelaine had died. *She* had sent her away.

Mom's hand fluttered to her throat. "Uh," was all she said.

"It was one thing for you and Dad to fight. But then having him take her." Anger and pain and a feeling that reminded me of ice coursed all through me.

"You heard that? You heard me wish away my daughter?"

"That accident was partially your fault." My mouth was a runaway train. I felt my heart clench up inside and I realized the words that I had let out, the words I had kept hidden inside me, were ones that I had never been sure of until right at this moment. And the funny thing was I regretted them all.

"I know it. I know it. It was my fault." Mom was crying now. "It was just that she always said whatever was on her mind. I thought it would be easier on me to have her away for a few days."

I had a flash of Madelaine goading Mom into buying a new pair of in-line skates. That argument had gone on for days, with Madelaine always saying something not quite nice. Now the skates sat on a shelf in the garage, still in the box, only used a few times.

"And she was getting to the age."

"The age?" My heart thumped, mostly from guilt. I wanted my words back. I hadn't meant for this to happen. And I hadn't expected her to accept Madelaine's death as her own responsibility, though I had wanted it.

"The argumentative stage." Tears rolled down Mom's face. "She was always fighting with me. And I couldn't take it from her and your dad, too."

Mom jumped to her feet, hitting the table. Soup sloshed over and onto the maroon tablecloth, making a dark splotch that looked like a cloud. A lone pea sat at the bottom of the cloud shape.

I jumped up too. Only one bite of egg roll remained and I pinched it between my fingers.

Mom and I faced each other now.

"We were fighting all the time," Mom said. Tears spilled down her cheeks. Chinese lanterns reflected in the wetness, making shiny tracks. "I wanted him to go. I wanted him to get out. I didn't think I cared if he lived or died. And then he did die. And he took my rebellious daughter with him. My baby with him. And I found out . . ." Mom cried so hard that people at the other tables stared. I could see the waitress hesitating near the brown swinging doors.

"Mom." I tried to take her hand but she wouldn't let me. She shook me away. "Mom. Stop. I didn't mean it." My voice was loud too.

"I found out some things don't matter. And if I had tried to work it out with him, they'd both be here now." She was almost yelling. "Some things don't matter. You work them out." She was fumbling for money. I saw her take two twenties from her wallet and throw them on the table—way too much money for what we had ordered. Then she was running toward the door.

At first I was too stunned to move. Then, thank goodness, my feet took off after her and I was calling, "Wait." But she didn't. Outside a wind had kicked up and a hot breeze blew, heavy with rain.

"Mom," I called.

She didn't answer me and she didn't head for the car, either. Instead she ran down the street, toward downtown.

I couldn't believe she was so fast. I mean for as old as she is, she was really moving. And I seemed so slow.

What have I done? I thought. Why had I said the words that I kept so private in my head? My eyes filled with tears. "Wait," I called.

Mom slowed down at the corner only because a

traffic light stopped her. I ran up beside her and reached for her arm. It had been so long since I had done that. So long since I had moved toward her.

A bit of rain splashed down around us. I could see it making quarter shapes on the sidewalk, even though all that lighted our way were the streetlamp and the red light.

Mom spun around when I touched her. Her face was wet with tears. Tears I had caused. Tears I had, in some strange way, wanted to see. "Don't you think," she said between clenched teeth, "that I've suffered enough? For more than a year I've carried this pain with me. One that wouldn't heal because I sent Madelaine away." Mom banged herself hard on the chest with her hands.

"Mom," I said.

"No!" she screamed, and that one little word seemed so full of anguish and drawn out. "You haven't helped me at all, Carolina. You've blamed me from the beginning. And I've known it."

"Mom," I said again, because what else could I say? She was right, I had given her the load, even if my mouth hadn't said so until tonight. Somebody need-ed this blame and I for sure couldn't carry it. Who was left but her? Dad and Madelaine were dead.

"I can't keep doing this alone," Mom said. She was crying full out now. And so was I. And it seemed that so was heaven, the way the big drops of rain came down so heavy and slow. "I just can't keep doing this alone."

I realized right then, under the streetlamp, in this beginning of a rain, that I couldn't do it alone either. I couldn't heal myself at all. And I wasn't so sure that there was anything that could heal me. But I did know this. Our family had been cut in half, and true as the dark around us, I only had my mom. And she only had me.

"I'm sorry." My voice wailed into the night air. "I'm sorry, I just miss them so much. I just miss them so much."

"So do I," Mom cried out. And it was like the two of us were standing on the street corner calling back the dead.

Loneliness made my heart feel too thin until Mom reached for me and pulled me in close to her. We stood there, hugging in the rain, which became lighter, then mistier, then finally was gone.

That night, after Mom and I got home from the restaurant, I sat in her office. In the corner, back by the bookcase, she had a big, comfortable chair left over from Dad. It was one he had had in his office in our old house.

I curled up in the recliner, tipping it back some. I stared at the ceiling, lit low, and remembered.

Then I decided maybe, just maybe, it was time to quit pulling away from my mother.

Chapter 19

The Catholic school was out of the question. So
was the high school in Daytona Beach. Mom said
I was staying in New Smyrna High because I had to
finish out the year. So I tucked my pride into my guts
somewhere and prepared for school the following
Monday, and for seeing Mara and Garret.

On Saturday morning I got up early and made
breakfast for my mother, something Dad used to do
on weekends.

I thought of my father as I made whole-wheat
pancakes for Mom and started the coffeepot. In the
other house, in the other kitchen that was all shiny
cream-colored tile, Dad would put on an apron
shaped like a giant fish and a tall chef's hat to

putter around the kitchen. He always wore a giant oven mitt, whether he really needed it or not. "For effect," he'd say. "It makes it seem like I'm working harder than I am."

His creations left a huge mess that he never cleaned up. It seemed, I remembered, that in the beginning Mom didn't mind cleaning up after the Saturday-morning fiasco. When had that changed?

Anyway, Dad would cook up everything, using all the pans, and then bring Mom a huge breakfast: hash browns, an omelet, muffins, orange juice and coffee. I smiled at the memory of the dishes stacked high and Mom eating in bed both Saturday and Sunday mornings.

I would be simple for her, compared to what Dad had made.

I put breakfast on a tray for the both of us, then hiked up the stairs to her room.

"Oh, Carolina," she said when I nudged her awake with my knee. "Look what you've done."

I grinned at her. There were some things I knew I couldn't do, as I stood there, tray in hand, near my mom, who looked young in the early-morning light. I couldn't change the accident. I couldn't make the gray hair go away. I couldn't alter the words she had said to Dad about Madelaine.

But I could be my mother's friend. And that's what I decided. The blaming, for me anyway, was over.

"I thought we could share the morning," I said.

"Sit up." She did and I set the tray over her. "But I get to choose the cartoons we watch."

"Cartoons?" Mom laughed. I climbed up in bed beside her and we never turned on the television. Instead, we sat in her bedroom and talked about superficial things: My schoolwork and hers. Being in the throes of autumn. Winter hanging just around the corner.

And she liked it. Breakfast, I mean. And the chatting. And miracle of miracles, so did I.

After breakfast I cleaned the kitchen, took Dad's camera—I mean *my* camera—and went to find some pictures like Ansel Adams had shot oh so long ago.

Of course, Florida isn't loaded down with too many waterfalls and huge rock formations, but this is New Smyrna and we do have the ocean.

I got on my bike and rode the five miles to the shoreline.

The beach was filled with people catching the last of the comfortable days before it would be too cold to do anything more than wander the shore. It was a hot day, but not as hot as summer would have made the air and sand and sun.

I walked at the edge of the water, barefoot, looking at the periwinkles the surf brought in. I only had black-and-white film in my camera, and really the periwinkles, so small and hidden in their rainbow shells, needed color film. But I took pictures of them anyway. The tide washed away the top layer of sand, and the periwinkles, exposed to the sun and air, dug

themselves back down, leaving tiny holes and sometimes bubbles.

I included my toes in a few shots, but mostly I
aimed at the tiny creatures before they made their
way into the wet sand.

Then I took pictures of the sand dunes, wind-
blown and smooth looking, before and after I
walked over them. I took pictures of a fisherman on
the jetty.

I used up three rolls of film. Afterward, I wrapped
my camera in the towel I had brought, and I lay down
on the beach to soak in the late-October sun.

A Note to You

*It's funny how I felt. Not all healed about the plane
crash, but healed in a mother-daughter way. She and I were
going to make it through this. And, as scary as it seemed to
reach out to her, at that moment I felt I would be able to do
it. And I really wanted to.*

Lying in the sand, I thought of Garret. "I can do
this," I said to myself. "I don't have to be his girlfriend anymore." And I almost believed myself.

When it was nearly time for dinner, I got on my
bike and headed home.

I went past the old park Dad and Mom and

Madeleine and I had played in when I was little. I circled it once, then after a bit dropped my bike in the thin grass. Here the oaks were crowded and the ground was sandy and covered with brown leaves.

I went to the swing where, it seemed, a hundred years ago I had sat on my father's lap and he had flown us to the sky.

"Don't go too high, Steven," Mom had said.

"Yes, Mommy," I shouted. "We're going to touch the leaves way up there."

"Don't be so paranoid, Amelia," Dad said.

In the swing next to us, Madeleine pumped too. "I'm racing you, Daddy."

"Go ahead and try to beat us," I hollered at Madeleine. "We've got swing engines on our butts and we're going to the sun."

Dad laughed, a deep rumbly laugh, and pushed us higher into the sky. It seemed the wind whistled in my ears.

"Steven." Mom made a nervous giggle, then climbed up on a third swing to join us in the fun.

The swing chains went slack, then taut, slack, then taut. We swung and swung, with Mom's voice and the wind and Daddy's laugh in my ears.

It had been a good day. It was a good memory. It made me feel warm and only a little bit lonesome.

It was after Sunday dinner that Garret came over.

Mom and I had settled down to play rummy when a knock sounded at the screen door.

"Who is it?" Mom called from the table where we had arranged ourselves.

"Garret Harrison. From next door."

Mom smiled.

I glanced at her. "I think he might be coming over to tell me he doesn't want to be my . . . friend anymore."

Mom's smile disappeared. "Oh," she said.

"Carolina," Garret called. "Can you come out for a few minutes?"

"I'm playing cards," I said.

"It won't take long."

"Should I go?" Mom asked.

A huge part of me wanted to send Mom out with a pen and a piece of paper to ask, "Can you write her a note?" But instead I said, "I better see what he wants."

"I've got some writing to do anyway," Mom said. "We'll play when you get back. Come get me out of my office when you're finished talking."

I nodded, laid down my hand of cards and went to meet Garret.

He stood at the door, his nose pressed onto the screen until he saw me coming.

"Carolina," he said, and his voice was low.

"What?" I was prepared to be angry, ready to shout

at him. But seeing him standing there, it softened up my heart.

"Come outside," he said, his voice still a whisper.

I unlatched the door and pushed it open. I didn't say anything but stepped onto the porch. A breeze blew in from the ocean.

"A storm's coming," Garret said. And as if to prove him right, the wind gusted up and tugged at my hair.

I crossed my arms in front of me and breathed in the deep ocean smell.

"Can we talk?" Garret asked.

"Sure," I said.

Garret looked at the porch floor, then back into my face. "I miss you," he said. "I miss you."

I didn't play cards with Mom that night after all. But instead I talked the storm to shore with Garret. We didn't bring up Mara and that was okay with me. Instead we talked a little about school and how it would be cold soon. Then we sat in the swing and after a moment or two Garret took my hand in his. And before he left that evening, he kissed me like never before, like maybe things were okay with us.

Chapter 20

I wasn't sure what woke me up later that night. Mom had turned off the air conditioner because of the storm and we opened all the windows to let the breeze in.

"It's less expensive this way," she said as we pushed the windows open together. "And I like the smell."

"Me too," I said. It had felt so nice being with her during the evening.

And Garret too.

When I went to bed, salt air smell thick in the night and tree frogs crying out for rain, I was pretty tired.

It hadn't been a dream. But whatever had woken

me set my heart and my hands to shaking. I lay in bed, flat on my back, and wondered.

The air was heavy and because of that, my yellow sheet felt sticky. I could see the glow from the soft hall lights, turned to their lowest setting.

"What?" I whispered. Was it Mom?

I sat up. And then I heard it again. A giggle. And a "Shhh."

At first I couldn't move. It was like I had been frozen there under a humid sheet. Then my heart began to pound, so hard I could feel it in my throat.

I started moving in slow motion. I sat up and swung my legs over the side of the bed. I put my feet on the cool floor and stood, stretching myself up. I felt like a ghost. I felt like I was a trespasser in my own house. I made my way around the bed.

There was the giggle again. Coming from outside.

"There's someone in the yard," I said, my voice low, my lips dry. I went to the window.

There they were. In Garret's front yard. Together.

The moon beamed down, casting a pure white light that was interrupted only by passing clouds that cast dark shadows across the yard.

"Garret," Mara said. She pulled him along closer to my yard.

"Please be quiet, Mara," Garret said.

"She won't wake up," Mara said. "She sleeps like a log."

A lie. A lie and Mara knew it. She knew I never

slept hard but woke at the slightest sound. Sleepovers had proved that to her. Dad's and Madelaine's deaths had made it even more so.

"I don't care," Garret said.

"Carolina," Mara said. Her voice was singsong. "I'm with your man. Only he's mine now."

"Stop it."

Mara threw her arms around Garret's neck. She kissed him and I saw him kiss her back. *I saw Garret kiss her back.*

I stepped away from the window and, almost without thinking, ran from my room, down the stairs and out of the house, leaving the front door open. The ground was wet with dew. I could feel dirt and grass clippings sticking to my feet.

My nightgown, thin and sleeveless, whispered around me as I ran, lightfooted, through the front yard. It was almost dreamlike the way I moved. I jumped the ditch and was out on the road, little rocks digging at my heels. But it didn't slow me any. In seconds I was in Garret's yard. I stood quiet and still in the privet hedge shadow.

"Carolina's not as wonderful as you think," Mara said. "You know her mom and dad were thinking of divorce before the plane crash."

What was she saying?

"She told me plenty of times she thought it was her fault. You know the whole divorce thing."

Garret freed himself from Mara's arms.

"Why do you say these kinds of things about her?" he asked.

"You wanted to know all about her. You said it yourself," Mara said. She shrugged and giggled again. Then she turned toward my window.

"I can't believe what a creep I am," Garret said.

Mara spun to face him. "You know, I'm getting sick of you saying that. Do you like me or not?"

A mosquito buzzed near my ear, and I didn't move at all, just waited for the answer.

But Garret said nothing.

Mara turned to my window again. "Carolina." Her voice seemed loud in the night.

"Don't," Garret said.

"Embarrassed? Are you embarrassed to be with me?"

Mara was angry. I could hear it in her voice.

"I don't want her to know."

"What? That we like each other? That we've kissed?"

A frog sounded near where I stood and for a moment I could see it in my mind, that thin-skinned, light green frog. Madelaine had really liked them.

"Carolina," Mara called.

"I said be quiet," Garret said.

"You know what," Mara said, still looking at my window. "I don't see what you like about her." And then she was calling again. "Carolina."

"Just exactly what is it that you want?" I said, stepping out of the dark.

Mara screamed and ran back to Garret, who looked at me wide-eyed.

"Other than Garret, what is it you want from me, Mara?" I asked. I moved along in the wet grass and then around Mrs. Harrison's berm of azaleas. It was almost like a horror show, only I didn't carry a knife.

"Carolina," Garret said.

"Do you really think I'm stupid?"

It only took Mara a moment to regain her composure. "Well, you are out here in your nightgown."

I ignored her comment. "I've known for a while that you've wanted to be with Garret. Everybody's known."

"Carolina," Garret said.

"Shut up." It felt to me like my blood was boiling. "I can't believe you. I knew *she* would do this," I said, pointing at Mara. "I've watched her steal boyfriends from lots of girls. But I didn't think you'd do it too, Garret. Especially after your words tonight."

"I . . ."

"I don't care." I could feel tears coming up into my throat, salty like an ocean storm. "I don't care anymore."

"Then go back inside," Mara said.

"I just wanted you to know I know," I said.

"We're not friends," Mara said. "We haven't been for a long time."

"As soon as you decided you wanted to be Garret's friend more than mine, things changed." I turned to Garret. "You are a liar," I said, and started away.

"No, Carolina," Garret said. He grabbed my arm. "I meant what I said tonight."

"Tonight?" Mara asked.

"I have missed you. I do miss you." Back behind Garret I saw a lightning bug flame. Another, hidden in the grass, lit up in answer.

I jerked free. "I said, you're a liar."

"Garret," Mara said, and she sounded shocked.

"I just haven't known how to say no," he said, and I knew he meant about Mara.

"Garret," Mara said again. "Do you mean . . . Fine," she said. "You tell me right now, Garret Harrison. Tell me right now, who do you want to be with?"

"Carolina, I'm sorry."

"Yeah, right," I said. I started for home again.

Garret ran up behind me and turned me around. "I'm sorry," he said. "I mean it."

"Tell her what she wants to know," I said. And then I was crying. "Tell her what she wants to know."

Mara came up, to push her way between us, but this time I stood my ground.

"She already knows," Garret said. "And so do you."

"Say it again," Mara said. "The way you do when we're kissing."

Garret looked down at the ground. Then he looked into my eyes. "I want to be with you, Carolina," he said.

◆ ◆ ◆

A Note to You

Did you think it would happen that way? I bet you didn't. You always thought everything was going to turn out bad, something that you got from Dad. Even in the movies. And I guess for the great big things in life, you were right, huh, Madelaine? But this time you would have been wrong.

Right then, with the moon washing over us, and Mara stomping away in the dark, I loved Florida's soft nights. Especially that one. The smells, the frog sounds, the moist air, the lightning bugs. Right at that moment I loved it so hard that there was an ache in my chest, for everything. Even the mosquitoes.

Epilogue

A Note to You

Mara dropped out of photography that Monday. For a while I never wanted to see her again, but believe it or not, I did start to miss her. We had had some pretty good times together.

As for Garret and me, I renamed him Poindexter. For a while, anyway. And we kind of started over. Just sitting in the swing and watching for fireflies. Doing schoolwork together. Going for walks and taking pictures. I didn't want to get caught again. You know, with my heart all out of joint.

The thing is this, Madelaine. My life keeps on going, you know. And as much as I miss you, I have to admit that I like the way things are heading. With Mom. And with Garret. With my whole self.

There's just one thing I really regret: that you didn't get to do any of this great stuff. No dating, no kissing, no graduating, no career. I mean you missed getting married and having kids of your own and grandkids, maybe, and then dying at a respectable time in your life. Garret was right, the whole thing really sucks.

I'm going to grow right past you, Older Sister, and that aches me.

But I plan on living enough for the two of us. I plan on enjoying the good times and making it through the tough times. Without you. Without Dad. And with or without fireflies.

If that's okay with you.

ABOUT THE AUTHOR

Carol Lynch Williams is the author of six books for young readers, including *The True Colors of Caitlynne Jackson,* an ALA Best Book for Young Adults, an ALA Quick Pick, and winner of the Golden Sower Award. Her most recent books for Delacorte Press were *If I Forget, You Remember,* a Notable Children's Trade Book in the Field of Social Studies, and *My Angelica,* which *Booklist* called "delightful." A four-time winner of the Utah Original Writing Competition, she lives in Mapleton, Utah, with her husband and their five children.